ASSASSINS FOR PEACE

Simon Larren Thrillers
Book Six

Robert Charles

SAPERE
BOOKS

Also in the Simon Larren Series

Nothing to Lose

Dark Vendetta

Mission of Murder

The Fourth Shadow

Arctic Assignment

Stamboul Intrigue

The Big Fish

Strikefast

ASSASSINS FOR PEACE

Published by Sapere Books.

24 Trafalgar Road, Ilkley, LS29 8HH
United Kingdom

saperebooks.com

ISBN: 978-1-80055-917-2

CHAPTER 1: THE FIRST STAGE

The man named Skoda checked the powerful rifle with a lover's hands, feeling for it a warmth that he had never felt for any woman. He sighted it for the third time upon the marble-columned entrance to the fashionable Tempest Club, directly opposite the green-lawned square below him, moving it gently to pinpoint every detail under the searching, magnified eye of the long telescopic sight. Briefly the fine crosshairs rested upon the broad chest of the grey-haired doorman who waited quietly in the shadows behind the open doors, and a tingle of fearful pleasure rustled through his thin, angular frame. Then reluctantly he lowered the rifle and stepped back.

Skoda had never killed a man before, and he wanted to, badly. But the men who had recognised his killing potential had not trained him to kill a mere doorman. He had to wait just a little while longer.

The June evening was still warm, and a straying pigeon from Trafalgar Square wandered contentedly over the patch of green that was enclosed by the stately facades of some of London's oldest buildings. The pulse of the city throbbed as always, but barely penetrated here in this sedate corner. There were one or two parked cars — a Mercedes, a Rolls Silver Phantom and a gleaming black Jaguar — but Skoda barely noticed them. He had no envy for fast cars; he couldn't even drive. He cradled all that he wanted in his pale, bony hands.

For a moment he watched the pigeon. The grey bird fluffed its feathers, then stretched its neck to peck hopefully at the neatly trimmed grass. Skoda had shot many pigeons in his boyhood, and he knew that he could cut the head from this one with just one shot. The thought was tempting, just a quick practice shot before the grand climax. He would like to indulge, but shook his head in sad movement, forbidding himself the pleasure.

He checked his wristwatch. Almost seven fifty-five. Any time now. He glanced back at the locked door behind him, but felt no fear that someone might attempt to get in. The room, together with the whole top floor of the building, was being redecorated, and so there was no reason for anyone to come up from below. The workmen had left two hours ago. He had passed them on the way up, avoiding direct contact and carrying the dismantled sections of the rifle in a carpenter's tool bag. It had been surprisingly easy, just as they had said it would be. He chuckled at the thought, for this club was almost as select and fashionable as the Tempest, and even his limited imagination could see the consternation of staff and members when they learned how easily it had been used.

Neither was he worried about the prospects of his own escape. Both staff and members of these clubs were invariably elderly, crippled with gout and flushed with port; no match for a fast-running man with a rifle to knock them aside or hold them back. He had only to dash down the stairs and out through the tradesmen's entrance at the back, where a fast car would be ready to whisk him away.

Skoda was an unthinking man, who believed in what he was told. And on top of that, the magnificent rifle they had given him had filled him with supreme confidence.

He waited patiently. The sound of a car made him stiffen, but when it appeared he relaxed. It was a large black taxi that stopped on one side of the square. Two men got out with slow, unhurried movements and disappeared into one of the buildings. The taxi drove off. The grey pigeon gave up its vain search for crumbs and flew off with an abrupt scuffle of wings. And then two dark blue helmets appeared: a constable and a sergeant. The two men walked slowly and stopped by the low railings close to the entrance to the Tempest Club. They, too, were waiting. Skoda knew then that his victim was coming — the police would not have been in attendance otherwise — and he smiled.

Five minutes later he heard another car approaching. The two policemen straightened to attention and took up their positions on either side of the entrance as a large black Wolseley slowed smoothly into the square. It stopped exactly in front of the Tempest Club, and the police sergeant moved smartly to open the rear door. Behind him the club doorman had moved forward from the shadows, but stood aside again as he saw that he was not needed.

Skoda drew a long, deep breath and carefully raised the rifle. For a moment the car blocked his view of the tall, grey-haired man who was now getting out of the back seat, but as the man straightened up and moved towards the club, his head and shoulders showed clearly above the car's roof. Skoda centred the crosshairs of the magnified sight on the back of the man's head.

He barely noticed the two Special Branch detectives who had also appeared from the car, and he had all but forgotten the two saluting policemen. He savoured the moment of absolute power following the grey-haired man up the three wide steps to the columned entrance, and then his curling finger gently squeezed the trigger.

The ringing crack of the rifle was a savage violation of the peaceful summer evening, and the Right Hon. Sir Howard Davies, K.B.E., V.C., M.P., and Prime Minister of Great

Britain, died instantaneously as the high-velocity bullet smashed into the back of his skull.

From the top floor window of the Bedford Hotel, Andre Jouvert could not see the front of the Tempest Club, but the road below him ran into the square, and from this angle he could see the open window opposite from which Skoda had fired the fatal shot. He was watching through the telescopic sight of a rifle that was almost identical to the one they had given Skoda. The only difference was that Jouvert's weapon was fitted with a specially designed silencer that would effectively muffle most of its sound.

Jouvert saw the quick smile that appeared on Skoda's face as he lowered his rifle and the echoes of that first shot died away, and the Frenchman knew that he had taught his pupil well. Skoda had not missed.

There was no emotion in him as he fired the second, unheard shot that killed the assassin who had thought him a teacher and a friend, and his only thought afterwards was that Skoda was a fool.

It had never occurred to Skoda to ask himself why they had needed him. A more intelligent man might have wondered why the expert marksman who had trained him could not have done the job for which he had been recruited equally well, but not Skoda. And he had naively believed they would take the risk that he could make a successful escape after the sound and direction of his shot had marked his position to the two armed Special Branch men who were the Prime Minister's constant bodyguard.

Jouvert smiled as he pictured the reactions of the two detectives once they had broken down the locked door of Skoda's room. They would break in tensed for a struggle, and all they would find was a corpse with an expression of shocked surprise on its thin, angular face. And by the time they had worked out the angle of the second shot it would be far too late.

Swiftly, but without any nervous haste, Jouvert dismantled his rifle, packing the sections neatly into the open briefcase that lay on the bed beside him. He had practised this task until he could complete it in thirty seconds flat. He zipped the leather case around the nestling parts, locked it, and was ready to leave. He paused another ten seconds to check the picture he presented in the wardrobe mirror, searching his suit for any tell-tale stains of oil. There were none, and he winked one eye at the bronzed, leathery reflection of his own face. Then he left the room and locked it behind him.

He walked briskly, but still without haste, the briefcase tucked in seeming innocence beneath his arm. He knew that by now police cars would be screaming past the hotel's main entrance on their frantic way to the scene of the crime, and so he chose to leave by a side exit into another street. A bright red Mini was parked a few yards away along the kerb, and he quickly climbed in, and a moment later he was driving away into the fast traffic of the West End.

Thirty minutes later Jouvert was reporting his success to a thick-set, fair-haired man named Henderson. They were both standing in a small, cramped and windowless room. The furniture consisted of a central table with three or four chairs, and the only outstanding item was the long-range radio transmitter that stood upon the second smaller table jammed into one corner. A third man sat before the radio, a cigarette sticking to his lower lip and a cheap paperback book open but forgotten in front of him.

He was the only other occupant of the room.

Henderson listened to the calm, matter-of-fact wording of Jouvert's report, and despite the fact that he was area controller here he could not suppress a brief, inner shiver. It was simple enough to plan an assassination as he had done, and perhaps simple enough to kill a stranger as Skoda had done, but to cold-bloodedly shoot down a man you had personally trained and instructed for the past six months — that was something different. It placed Jouvert in a special class of his own.

However, Henderson kept his feelings hidden, and when Jouvert had finished he asked curtly, "Are you certain that Skoda is dead?"

Jouvert eyed him coldly. "There is no doubt."

Henderson smiled, perhaps a little too quickly. "Then the first stage of the operation is successfully completed. There was a newsflash on the radio five minutes ago. It said that the Prime Minister died instantly."

"And now?" Jouvert asked.

"Now we keep our heads down for a couple of days, and then we'll return to Paris. Our part in the organisation is finished. It is up to the other branches now." He turned to the man seated in front of the radio and said briskly, "Radio Zurich and report that phase one is completed."

The operator nodded and swivelled his chair to face the set.

CHAPTER 2: THE SULTRY STRIP

Simon Larren saw the newsflash announcing the Prime Minister's death on the television set in his flat in Rushlake Terrace. He was deriving some wry amusement from one of the current crop of gimmick-laden spy films when the screen was interrupted by the grave face and hushed tones of the newsreader. Automatically he switched off the electric razor in his hand — for he was watching through the open bathroom door as he shaved — and slowly moved back into the living room.

The announcement was brief: simply that the Prime Minister had followed his usual Friday evening habit of arriving to dine at his fashionable London club, and had been shot down on the steps by a gunman firing from the top floor window of the equally fashionable Centaur Club opposite.

There was no more, and as the newsreader quietly promised more reports as they came in, Larren released his feelings in an explosive curse. It was partly an expression of angry disgust at a senseless killing, and partly the reaction of a man who realised that he personally could be caught up in the security panic that must follow.

The screen went blank, and after a moment Larren turned sharply back into the bathroom. He flicked the razor back into life and deftly cleaned the last rough edge of his now tightened jaw. When he had finished he zipped the razor into its leather case, pulled off the towel that was knotted around his middle and strode naked to the bedroom.

His black evening suit was laid out ready on the bed, but now he ignored it, instinct telling him that there would be no nightclubbing tonight. Instead he took a dark grey suit from the wardrobe. It was single-breasted, smart but not too expensive, the kind of suit that would not seem too out of place in the widest variety of surroundings. He chose a cream shirt and a grey tie with a threaded pattern of red silk, and dressed swiftly. He was still knotting the tie when the telephone rang.

Larren returned to the living room to pick it up, knowing in advance that the call came from Whitehall, and that the little man who called himself simply "Mr Smith" would be on the other end of the line. Smith's voice was precise as always, but now there was a ring of controlled anger in his tone.

"Larren, you've heard the news?"

"Five minutes ago," Larren answered. "Do you want me to come up?"

"No." Smith's voice was curt. "Get over to Kingston. You'll find Adrian Cleyton sitting in a green Austin van opposite Limewood Gardens, just off the Sutherland Road. I want Cleyton back here. You'll relieve him."

"That's all?"

"That's all. Cleyton will give you the details."

"I'm on my way," Larren said, but even as he spoke he heard the click as Smith hung up.

Slowly Larren replaced the silent receiver on its cradle, and he realised that Smith was shaken, or at least as shaken as his ice-cold brain could ever be. Britain's internal security was the direct responsibility of Counter-Espionage, and the assassination of the P.M. was going to have strong repercussions throughout the department. However, there was no time to waste in wondering about the top-level confusion that must now be rushing through Whitehall and Scotland Yard, and turning swiftly Larren returned to his bedroom.

It took him two minutes to finish dressing, and five seconds to decide against carrying his Smith & Wesson .38. He didn't like the discomfort of a shoulder holster, and in any case he was more than capable with the light throwing knife that was concealed inside the breast of his jacket. He paused only to switch off the television and left the flat, hurrying down the stairs to his white MG sports car, which was parked outside.

Within a few minutes he was out on Baker Street, turning south and heading by the most direct route to Chelsea Bridge. He was held up briefly at Hyde Park Corner, but apart from that he made good time, driving confidently and exceeding the speed limit as much as he dared. Once south of the Thames he made better time and drove straight to Kingston.

It took him another ten minutes to find Sutherland Road, in one of the more expensive residential areas, and he drove more slowly until he spotted the green Austin van. It was the only green van parked in the road, and Larren swung the MG close against the kerb behind it, braking and switching off his engine. There was a quiet side road of neat semi-detached houses just a few yards ahead, and Larren read the name LIMEWOOD GARDENS on a plaque fixed on the corner of the first garden wall. He left the MG and walked forward to the van.

Adrian Cleyton smiled briefly, then relaxed again as Larren swung into the seat beside him. Cleyton was a younger man than Larren, slim and supple with the figure of a highly trained ballet dancer. He had soft brown eyes and dark, almost girlish lashes. He could have been mistaken for a shy homosexual, but Larren knew that he was nothing of the sort. Cleyton had the skill and hidden strength to tackle a judo champion at his own game, which — together with the ability of a born actor, his disarming charm, and a fluent mastery of at least six foreign languages — made him one of Counter-Espionage's top agents.

He said quietly, "Hello, Simon. You didn't waste much time."

"Smith sounded urgent," Larren explained. "He wants you back in Whitehall, Cleyt."

"I gathered that. Did he give you any details?"

"No, but I guess it's something to do with the P.M. You know that he's been assassinated? He was shot down on the steps of the Tempest Club."

"I heard the newsflash." Cleyton's face was grim. "I don't know any more."

"Neither do I." Larren was unsmiling.

"But what's this all about? I'm supposed to relieve you."

"Routine observation," Cleyton explained briefly. "A man named Henry Mallory. He lives at number six, Limewood Gardens. He's a Member of Parliament, a rather minor one. A strong ban-the-bomb supporter, member of the Campaign for Nuclear Disarmament, etcetera. He stands up and protests every time the Government announces any new expenditure on defence or arms. In his early days he had dealings with the Communist Party, and although he's now supposed to be wholly Socialist he's inclined to be chummy with any extremist group that promises El Dorado, however impractical. We've been keeping a paternal eye on him from time to time, as we do with anyone in an influential position who starts to dabble with these extremist fringe groups, and just lately we've had reason to believe that he might be mixed up in something a bit more melodramatic than usual. Smith had his phone tapped for a short period and found that he was making some peculiar, guarded calls to different call boxes throughout London. There was nothing definite, but it was felt that Henry Mallory would bear a closer watch. Smith decided on round-the-clock observation for three days, to be called off if nothing had turned up at the end of it. This is the second day."

Cleyton had passed over a postcard-sized photograph as he talked, and Larren studied the picture of a bluff-faced man in his late fifties. The man had moderately thick dark hair, greying slightly at the temples, and a thick, military-style moustache.

"He's five foot six tall, and weighs just over eleven stone." Cleyton filled in the rest of the details. "He was sitting in the House of Commons throughout the day, but right now he's at home."

Larren glanced up. "If he was sitting in the House then he could be in a position to have known whether the P.M. would be working on tonight. He could have passed word that there was nothing to stop Sir Howard keeping his usual Friday evening dinner date at the Tempest."

Cleyton smiled. "Nothing's impossible, but I don't think Mallory had anything to do with today's business. It'll probably turn out to be the work of a single crank rather than an elaborate plot by some secret political group. But until we're sure, every police and intelligence department in the country will be double-checking on all the shady and oddball organisations on their files, and everyone connected, or even suspected of having connections with any of those groups will come under the microscope. And Mallory does come under that general classification. That's why Smith wants the watch on him to be continued."

Larren grimaced. "Is there any indication as to what kind of people he might be playing with?"

"If there is, then Smith hasn't told me. But I don't think there's anything definite. Those phone calls are all that we really have to go on, and probably it will all turn out to be a false alarm, exaggerated by our own nasty minds. It's been drab routine so far, and will most likely stay that way. Henry Mallory will be proved as innocent as a babe in arms, and the odds are that they'll have caught the P.M.'s killer before I can get back to report." His own words seemed to remind him of the need for haste, and Cleyton finished briskly, "There's a wife and a twenty-eight-year-old daughter in the house with him, but that's all. Just keep a check on any visitors and follow him if he goes out. You've got night glasses and radio here under the dashboard. Give number six a look over now and again, and report negative every two hours. I doubt if you'll have anything else to report. They're using the Watchdog routine again. You call Watchdog Master, and identify yourself as Watchdog M. The M stands for Mallory."

"Understood," Larren said briefly. "You'd best take my car and get moving. But bear in mind that it's not Government property to be wrecked at will."

Cleyton smiled as he accepted the keys of the MG, and wished him luck as he got out of the van. A few moments later the white sports car pulled past and accelerated away on its return journey to the centre of London. Larren watched the tail lights disappear, then reached for the night glasses.

Without leaving the van he could see down the side road opposite that was Limewood Gardens, and with the aid of the powerful glasses he could cover the whole frontage of number six. There was a light behind the drawn curtains of the main living-room window, and the household had obviously settled down for the night. Larren could not see through the curtains, and after briefly scanning the front garden and surrounds he replaced the glasses in their leather case. There was a street light just outside the front gate of number six, and even without the glasses he would be able to see if anyone entered or left the house. He leaned back in the darkness of the van and settled himself for a long vigil.

He made two radio reports, one at ten p.m. and one at midnight after the last square of light had appeared and then vanished from the upper floor of the Mallory home. On the second call he was told to discontinue negative reports, and realised that Watchdog Master had far more important problems on its mind. He decided sourly that as far as the main job was concerned, this time he wasn't even on the sidelines.

He was relieved at seven the following morning when two pseudo-workmen arrived to dig up the pavement outside number six, but by late evening he was back in his old position in the green van. He learned that Henry Mallory had not once left the house, and that the agent who had been on hand to follow if the workmen had reported his leaving had had a wasted day.

However, the watch was to continue. Cleyton's assumption that the assassination of Sir Howard Davies had been the work of an isolated crank had been swiftly proved wrong, and today the whole country knew that there had been a second assassin. The morning's newspapers had screamed the story of how the Prime Minister's Special Branch shadows had rushed to the top floor of the Centaur Club with two policemen in close support, only to find that the killer was already dead. Scotland Yard experts had managed to establish that the second shot had come from the window of room 79 on the upper floor of the Bedford Hotel, which overlooked one of the streets leading into the square, but by then the second assassin had had a clear hour in which to make his escape. One of the papers had described it as a classic case of shooting round corners and neatly removing the middleman.

The papers had also carried a crude sketch identikit picture that Scotland Yard men had coaxed from the shocked hotel staff who had attended room 79, together with a description that Larren, in company with every other policeman and intelligence agent in Great Britain, now knew by heart. They were looking for a black-haired man with a thin narrow face, a face that was leathery and sunburned as though he had spent several years in the tropics. He was approximately five feet eight inches tall and approximately thirty-five years of age. Last seen wearing a dark blue suit, white shirt and dark tie, and carrying a black leather briefcase. He had a slight Continental accent and was possibly of French birth.

That was all that the papers knew, and Larren doubted whether Scotland Yard or Counter-Espionage knew very much more. The only definite thing was that the assassination had been well planned and was no one-man job. Some kind of organisation was involved, and so the screw was still being tightened on every sub-movement and splinter group that was known, political or otherwise, and on all their possible sympathisers. And Henry Mallory, although a long way down, was still on the list.

The evening became dusk again as Larren watched the house, and he began to feel, as Cleyton had done, that watching Mallory was a waste of time. He grew bored, for he had received little practice in showing the patience needed for a routine observation job like this one. Like Cleyton, Simon Larren had his own special qualities that would normally lift him above the rut of routine. He was perhaps the only natural killer under Smith's command. Cleyton and most of the others could kill if they had to, but none of them liked it, whereas

Larren was a lone operator who listed his choice of allies as silence, darkness and a knife. He had been taught to kill by the Special Operations Executive during the wartime years, and had learned the animal thrill of pitting his skill and capabilities against greater odds. Now Smith used him for violent assignments, the ones that a more squeamish man might not survive, and so far he had always come back. This job was outside his normal sphere, but he knew that the department was working flat out to catch the people behind the assassination of Sir Howard Davies, and that he had only been given it to release Cleyton, who was a better investigating agent.

Despite being resigned to a dull evening, he remained alert, and missed nothing when the door of number six abruptly opened two hours later. Light spilled out on to the front path, and Larren automatically raised his night glasses to study the man who now stood in the doorway, fumbling with his coat. The powerful lenses picked out the bluff face and thick moustache that matched the photograph in Larren's pocket, and he knew that this was Henry Mallory.

Mallory paused in the doorway for a moment. A grey-haired woman, obviously his wife, stood behind him, and he kissed her lightly on the temple before turning along the front of the house towards the garage. Larren watched him backing out his car, a large saloon that could have been a Zodiac or a Zephyr, and decided that the evening might not be quite so dull after all. He doubted very much whether a man who could kiss his wife so lovingly could be setting off for some dark and dangerous rendezvous, but trailing him would pass the time more easily.

Larren replaced his glasses and contacted Watchdog Master with the information that he was about to follow Mallory's car.

He received a disinterested reply to go ahead, but knew that there would be hell to pay if he adopted the same attitude and lost his quarry, however harmless Mallory's night trip might be.

A moment later the large saloon turned towards him from Limewood Gardens, slowing to enter the main road and then swinging wide to get past the green van. Larren kept his face away as Mallory's headlights bathed his windscreen, but he noted the licence number and the fact that the car was a grey Zephyr. He let Mallory get past the first curve in the road that hid him from sight, then swiftly started the van and did a sharp U-turn in pursuit.

He had Mallory's car in sight again in less than a minute, for Mallory was driving carefully whereas the engine of the van had been turned by experts and was capable of unexpected speeds. Larren held the van back once he had renewed contact, and allowed two passing cars to get between himself and the grey Zephyr. There was plenty of traffic once they started up Kingston Hill, and as they were all going the same way, towards central London, there was little likelihood of Mallory realising that he was being followed.

Mallory chose to follow the A3 for most of the way, and when he finally turned off to head across Westminster Bridge, Larren was still behind him. They passed beneath the shadow of Big Ben, then along Whitehall, and although it was now past ten o'clock there were plenty of lights burning in the Houses of Parliament, as well as in the upper windows of the Foreign Office and Scotland Yard. Larren's unsmiling mouth became a little grimmer as the lights emphasised that one of the greatest killer-hunts in English history was still taking place. He closed up slightly on the grey car ahead, determined to do his little bit, even if it was only the patient elimination of a not-very-likely possibility.

They circled Trafalgar Square, with Larren again easing back to let a large taxi slide in front and conceal him as they were caught by the traffic lights. They continued down Charing Cross Road, but after crossing Shaftesbury Avenue Mallory suddenly turned left into the square mile of Soho.

A few moments later Mallory found a parking meter and stopped. Larren swore softly as he realised that he had to drive on past the man, but Mallory appeared to take no notice of the passing van as he got out of his car. Larren turned sharp right at the next opportunity and swung the van into an enclosed mews yard that was pointedly labelled PRIVATE PARKING ONLY. He wedged the van between a Sunbeam Rapier and a tank-sized Daimler, locked it and hurried briskly back the way he had come.

The grey Zephyr was empty when he reached it, and so was the street in which it was parked. Larren burst into a sprint that took him to the next corner in record time, and glanced searchingly right and left. There was only one retreating figure in sight that was of the right height and weight, and without hesitation he hurried in pursuit. The man was headed back towards Shaftesbury Avenue, and as Larren drew closer the light from an overhead club sign showed him that it was Mallory. Larren risked falling back again and breathed a sigh of relief.

For the next five minutes he trailed Mallory on foot, past the coffee bars and jazz clubs, and the windows full of sexy magazines and semi-pornographic books. A clip-joint girl gave him an appraising look as she leaned against a curtained doorway, but she didn't bother to smile. Squirls of shoddy neon flickered suggestively above the heads of passers-by, hinting at sinful pleasures in hidden corners. Two long-haired youths argued in a pub doorway, and a mincing boy went past with pale face and red mouth, and an uncaring smile that spelled some inner joy. Larren recorded it all, but never once lost sight of Henry Mallory.

His quarry stopped suddenly, looking around him for the first time. Larren carried on walking slowly, covering another ten yards before he stopped in a doorway to light a cigarette. Mallory moved on, and Larren watched out of the corner of his eye as the man turned into a brightly lit opening that threw a pool of glaring yellow on to the pavement. There was a neon sign above it, but from this angle Larren could not make out the words. Mallory hesitated for another second and then disappeared.

Larren gave him two minutes, then approached the spot. Two large placards adorned with pinned photographs of smiling nudes framed the entrance through which Mallory had passed, and above the neon sign flashed the words THE SULTRY STRIP.

Larren stared thoughtfully. He supposed that perhaps it wasn't all that uncommon for a seemingly happily married man to show an interest in a strip club, but even so it struck a note that was out of character. The general public liked to think of passionate idealists being proved as secret lechers, but they rarely were.

"Care to see the show, sir? Continuous performance. All lovely girls."

A sexless face with a pale brassy smile spoke the words from a tiny pay desk window just inside the doorway. The smile suggested more than the words, but Larren was under no delusions. If it had not been imperative that he keep track of Henry Mallory he would have smiled cynically, but instead he moved into the doorway and asked how much.

"Fifteen shillings, sir. And well worth it."

Larren saw now that the face was male and attempting a sly man-to-man camaraderie. He paid for his ticket and followed directions through a curtained doorway and up a flight of bare wooden stairs. The stairway was narrow, and in places the yellow plaster had peeled away from the walls. There was an open doorway facing the first-floor landing, with the sound of rhythmic music coming from inside. The stairs continued upwards at a reversed angle, and a Biro-written postcard tacked to the wall read simply: NEXT FLOOR. YOUNG MODEL. LITTLE NANCY.

Larren entered the darkened clubroom, and another bloodless young man came forward to tear his ticket. To his left, above the heads of the silent audience, was a cramped stage where a bored young woman was stripping listlessly to recorded music. Two cheap spotlights gave a sickly whiteness to her bare flesh as she danced, and her eyes were fixed high on the smoke-filled ceiling. Most of her clothes were already draped over the chair that stood on the stage behind her, and she wore only a diminutive G-string. She swayed sinuously as her fingers caressed her own body, stroking her large breasts with frigid detachment.

Larren barely spared her a glance. He closed his eyes to accustom them to the gloom, avoiding the one bright spot of the stage, and then he searched among the audience for his quarry.

But Henry Mallory was not there.

CHAPTER 3: LOVE FOR SALE

Larren moved quietly behind the seated audience and approached halfway towards the stage down the narrow, sloping aisle that ran by the far wall. From this angle he could see most of the watching faces, and only the first few rows still had their backs towards him. No one seemed to notice his searching gaze, for all their eyes were upon the stage where the dancer had turned away from them and was making a teasing play of drawing the tiny G-string from between her legs. Her smooth shoulders and bare buttocks twitched spasmodically in time to the throb of the music, and she was humming an absent-minded tune as she worked.

Larren's gaze held each dim, captive face in turn, but after another minute he knew that Henry Mallory had definitely given him the slip.

The dancer on the stage turned slowly to face the clubroom, her shoulders swaying dreamily from side to side. Her hands were clasped coyly in front of her in the pose well beloved by men's magazines. She teased for another moment, then spread her hands to reveal herself as the music stopped. She smiled vaguely as she posed, and then the curtains trundled across the stage and hid her from view. By then Simon Larren had ascertained that there was no secondary exit from the clubroom, except possibly behind the stage, and that consequently the only way that Mallory could have gone was to have bypassed this room and continued up the stairs.

Thoughtfully Larren shifted to the back of the room again. He recalled the "young model" card that had been pointing up the stairs, but again it seemed out of character that Mallory should be indulging in sin. And then another thought registered; surely the "young model's" customers would be most likely to visit her after seeing the show, not before. Mallory's actions were not only out of character; they were in the wrong order.

Suddenly Larren knew that shadowing Henry Mallory was no longer a routine matter of elimination, and no longer a waste of time. For if Mallory was mixed up with some secret or criminal organisation, then here was the ideal cover for a regular meeting place. Anyone who recognised him, or followed him, would automatically ascribe his furtive movements to the more obvious motives, and the same would apply to his colleagues. In fact, Larren realised that if Mallory had sat and watched the strip show for half an hour before making his way up to the next floor, then he would most probably have relaxed his suspicions and simply waited to take up the trail when the man descended once more.

Larren decided then that he too would pay a visit to Little Nancy.

He quietly left the clubroom as a voice behind the curtains announced the presentation of Madeline, a poor but beautiful Parisienne, forced to walk the streets for her living. The curtains parted to reveal a young brunette in a tight black skirt and sweater. Behind her was a cheap backcloth showing the Eiffel Tower and in the background a female voice huskily sang the words of "Love for Sale".

Larren thought the song wryly appropriate as he started up the second flight of narrow, uncarpeted stairs. As he climbed he smoothed both hands briefly down his thighs, a reflex movement to dry the sweat from his palms which he made without thinking whenever the prospect of action seemed imminent. A strong instinct was telling him that his suspicions were on the right track, and for a moment he regretted that he had not brought the Smith & Wesson.

The staircase finished at a second small landing, and there was one closed door. Beside it was a bell push, together with another Biro-written card: YOUNG MODEL. PLEASE RING. Larren rang the bell.

From below the words of the song drifted upwards, carried by a cloud of cigarette smoke from the darkened clubroom where Madeline was slowly unzipping her hip-hugging skirt.

"She's got love for sale … Fresh love, and unspoiled love … Only slightly soiled love … She's got love for sale…"

There was a movement behind the door, and then it opened. A young blonde woman smiled up at him, her red lips fixed in the age-old parody of welcome. She was small, despite her high heels, and wore a tight skirt and a loose blouse.

"Hello, love," she greeted him. "Do come in."

Larren gave her what he hoped was the expected embarrassed smile, and stepped warily past her into a tiny, cupboard-like anteroom. To his left was a small side-room, and his gaze automatically probed through the open door. There were two faded armchairs, but otherwise the room was empty, and there was no alternative exit. Larren expected to be told to wait in there, but instead the woman smiled again and led him through a second door into her bedroom.

The furniture was unimpressive, just a shabby bed, two wooden chairs and an old sideboard. There was a closed door in the far wall. Larren knew that Henry Mallory must have passed through that far door, for there was nowhere else that the man could have gone.

The blonde woman had turned to face him and he realised that this was Little Nancy, and not the maid as he had first supposed, and now he found himself in a quandary. "It's two pounds, dear," she told him cheerfully. "Is that all right?"

"It's all right." Larren made a slow show of fumbling for his wallet and stalled for time. The set-up was wrong, for there was no maid to welcome visitors, just the woman herself, and he was convinced that this was a front. With most of her visitors the woman would go through her performance, but at certain times a very few would be passed straight through that closed door, and somehow Larren had to be one of the few.

The woman had taken off her blouse, but now she paused and looked at him strangely. "What's the matter, dear? Not shy, are you?"

Larren hesitated with his wallet in his hand. "No, just cautious. What's behind that door?"

"Nothing, dear. Why?"

Larren made another pretence at hesitation. "I like to know. I don't want any photographs. I'm not a mug. I won't fall for blackmail."

"Don't be silly, dear. There's nothing like that."

Larren stepped back a pace, still playing his chosen part. "Show me," he insisted. "I want to see behind the door first."

"I can't. It's kept locked." The woman's voice had become flat and just a little nervous. Her smile had slipped, and Larren knew that she was flustered. The door was important.

"Look, dear, stop worrying." The forced smile returned. "There's nothing wrong. I've got some nice pictures I can show you if you like. Perhaps they'll help you." She gave a knowing wink and turned to the battered sideboard, pulling open a top drawer.

For the moment the side of her neck was perfectly exposed as she sorted through half a dozen packets of photographs, and automatically Larren decided his next move. If he had missed and the woman had screamed he knew that he would never have convinced the police that he was not a sex-killer and a maniac, but he was too well practised to miss. He stepped forward and struck swiftly with the edge of his stiffened hand, and Little Nancy sagged unconscious into his arms, a scattering of obscene pictures falling from her slack fingers.

Carefully Larren lifted her on to the shabby bed, then stood silent for a moment with his senses alert. There was nothing to be heard except the faint music that throbbed up from the strip club below, and he rubbed the cutting edge of his palm with gentle satisfaction.

He crossed to the closed door and listened, then gingerly twisted at the knob. The door was unlocked and he eased it open. He knew that he had operated in silence and that only his initial conversation could have been heard, but even so he moved warily. Any step at this stage was a risk, but he could neither see nor hear beyond this door, and so he had to gamble that there was no one immediately behind and pass through it.

It was a gamble that failed. There was darkness beyond, and he could see nothing through the slender crack he had made, then abruptly the door was yanked forwards out of his hand. He thrust back instinctively, but fast though he was his assailant was faster. He caught a brief glimpse of the leathery face behind the swinging cosh, and then the blow struck home directly between his eyes and blackness crashed over him in a solid flood.

Henderson jerked away from the peephole that looked directly down upon Little Nancy as she sprawled slackly on her bed, and flicked down the light switch close by his side. Behind him, Henry Mallory stood with his back pressed against the wall, close to the radio operator who sat tensely by his set. In the doorway Andre Jouvert turned confidently to face them, standing splay-legged and idly twirling the wicked black cosh.

"Drag him inside," Henderson said harshly. "Andrews, give him a hand."

The radio operator nodded, removing his earphones and crossing the room to help Jouvert with the slumped figure of Simon Larren. They dragged Larren inside and rolled him on to his back. His eyes were closed, and a thin trickle of blood ran down into his eyebrow from the ugly bruise that had appeared in the centre of his forehead.

Jouvert spared him a glance and said, "What about the girl?"

"Nancy!" Henderson stepped through the door and looked down at the still figure on the bed. "Leave her there. The familiar surroundings will help her when she comes round. Just lock the outer door in case of any more customers, and take in the cards."

Jouvert nodded; he slipped the cosh into his belt and fastened his jacket over it before moving to obey. Henderson turned and went back into the room where Simon Larren lay across the floor. Mallory was now standing over him, his face pale and frightened.

"I told you," he said. "I told you someone was following me. They're on to us already."

"And you led him straight here." Henderson struggled to keep the useless anger out of his tone, but he failed to hide his disgust. "You may have betrayed the lot of us, just because you're too scared to keep your stupid head."

Mallory edged away, retreating from the harshness of the other man's face. "What do you expect?" he demanded. "That I'm going to sit there and let them pick me up while the rest of you make a clean getaway? I stayed away before the job, but now that it's done and our part is finished, then I'm entitled to get out as much as the rest of you. I'm —"

He took another step back as he saw the breaking fury in Henderson's eyes, but was brought up to a solid stop as he bumped into the unmoving Andrews. His heart was thumping, and he flinched as though he expected one of them to strike him.

The thick-set Henderson took another grip on his temper and said flatly, "There was no need for you to make any kind of escape at all. Even if they did have suspicions there was nothing that they could prove against you. You didn't even contact us yesterday; it was your silence that told us that Davies would almost certainly be at the Tempest. You were in the clear and now you've landed yourself in a bloody mess." He stopped, and scuffed a hand through his sandy fair hair in a gesture of violent exasperation. "Take another look at him," he said. "Are you sure it's the man who was following you?"

Mallory straightened his lapels, as though self-consciously preparing himself to face the House, and moved tentatively forward. He looked down at Larren for the second time and nodded.

"He's the one. He was watching from a green van parked at the end of the road outside my house. I was expecting something of the sort, or I probably shouldn't have noticed. There were some workmen directly outside my house today, and they first made me suspicious. They kept hanging the job out, and nobody came to supervise them or see how they were getting on. When they left I went upstairs and used binoculars from behind the curtains to see who had taken their place. I saw this chap in his van, and when he was still there an hour later I was sure. That's when I decided to come here." He paused weakly. "I thought — I thought I'd lost him in the traffic coming into London."

"You damned fool," Henderson snarled. "Why the hell didn't you go to Westminster today as you would normally have done? With Parliament holding an emergency meeting over the death of the Prime Minister it was the expected thing for you to do. You must have made yourself obvious by staying away. That's probably what put them on to you."

"For God's sake, man, I felt ill. Surely you can see that I couldn't face the House after yesterday." Mallory cried the words in anguish, pushing forward earnestly. "I can never sit in Parliament again, knowing what I've done. I know it was necessary, but I've hated myself for the part I had to play in doing it. That's why I've got to escape. I've got to start somewhere new."

He broke off and turned away as Jouvert returned. Henderson looked at the man, of whom even he was a little afraid, and Jouvert nodded briefly. He tossed the two printed YOUNG MODEL cards on the table and then glanced down at Larren. "Have you searched him yet?"

"No." Henderson shook his head wearily. "You'd better do it now."

Jouvert nodded calmly and knelt beside the unconscious Larren. He checked for a shoulder holster, and seemed surprised that he did not find one, but when he fished out Larren's wallet his fingers encountered the flat hilt of the knife that was reached through the inside pocket. He drew it out and whistled approvingly, balancing the blade on his hand.

"Very neat," he observed. "And well concealed. I almost missed it. Our friend strikes me as a professional." He stood up, flicked the knife into the nearby tabletop, and proceeded to flip through the contents of Larren's wallet. He found the photograph of Henry Mallory and passed it on to Henderson.

The thick-set man stared at it for a moment. "So there's no mistake," he said. "Our *friend*, as you call him, was trailing Mallory."

"I've already told you that," Mallory said desperately. "They're on to me. You've got to get me out of the country."

Henderson watched him for a moment, recognising the signs of panic in the older man's bluff face. There were traces of sweat at the corners of his mouth, and the stiffness seemed to have gone out of the clipped military moustache. Mallory was a worried man. He had lost his nerve.

"All right," said Henderson. "We'll take care of your unwanted friend for you. And after that I think we can arrange to get you to Morocco."

CHAPTER 4: OF FIRE AND COURAGE

"And after that I think we can arrange to get you to Morocco."

The last of Henderson's words sank slowly like clumsy leaden weights through the thick mud of Larren's returning senses. His brain was a primeval swamp where the first dawnings of life were only just beginning to stir, crawling sluggishly through darkness towards the light. He fought against the pain of birth, a pain that crashed and echoed like the striker of a giant bell inside the confines of his skull, but the animal instinct for life could not be denied. His brain lifted from the lower depths of unconsciousness and the second voice came more sharply, piercing through the thinning layers of space and time.

"He's coming round. We'd better tie him up before he gets too lively."

Henderson looked down as Jouvert spoke, and he nodded in agreement. "Andrews," he ordered, "bring some of that electrical wiring over here."

The radio operator nodded. His sallow face was expressionless, and a stub of cigarette again clung to his lower lip. He fetched the coil of red-flexed wiring from the table by his set, and brought a pair of pliers at the same time. Jouvert took them from him.

"I'd better tie him," the Frenchman said. "I don't trust this character."

Andrews made no protest at the implied doubt to his own ability. He was a one-job man, and his job was the radio. And in any case, Jouvert was not the kind of man with whom you could protest or argue. He simply watched as Jouvert cut off two lengths of the wire and efficiently secured Larren's wrists and ankles. As a final measure he tied Larren's thumbs and then used the last of the trailing wire to draw his feet up to meet them. It was, Andrews had to admit, a very professional job.

Larren regained full consciousness as Jouvert worked, but by then it was too late to resist. The great bell still sounded resoundingly in his skull, each stroke of pain blotting out all thought and reason, but gradually the blows began to decrease. A nonchalant foot rolled him over, half on to his side and half on to his back because of his arms and legs pulled behind him, and with an effort he opened his eyes. On the second attempt he got them to stay open, and began to register the faces that regarded him from above.

Mallory he recognised instantly, but Henry Mallory was unimportant now. It was the remaining three faces he filed away in his memory. Andrews he noted briefly, for there was an attitude of detachment about Andrews that would always mark him as a minor cog in any wheel; he was unconcerned now, simply waiting to see what the others would decide. Henderson was a different class altogether; Larren saw the angry frown on the bigger man's face, and sensed the dominance in the thick-set figure. He marked the fair-haired man as one of importance. And then he forgot Henderson as his gaze found the leathery face he had seen too late behind the falling cosh.

The man fitted the description that was forged into its own special compartment in Larren's brain. The black hair, and the narrow, sun-bronzed face, dark with the Gallic lines that betrayed his French parentage, matched perfectly to the identikit sketch that had gazed from the front page of every newspaper in the land, and Larren knew that he had found the second assassin who had taken part in the murder of Sir Howard Davies.

"All right, now that you've had a good look at us, why don't you start by telling us who you are?"

Larren looked back at Henderson as the big man spoke. His head had cleared a little now, and he made an effort to make his voice sound blustering as he answered, "What the devil is this — some kind of blackmailing stunt? I had the feeling it was. That woman out there —"

"Stuff it!" Jouvert told him bluntly. He showed the photograph of Mallory that he had taken from Larren's wallet. "We've already found this. And besides, there's a peephole in the wall. We saw the way you handled Nancy. You were too good at it."

Larren swore inwardly, realising that he had made a bad blunder in retaining the photograph. Now it was pointless to bluff, and he said sourly, "So there was a peephole. I'll bet that's given you hours of happy viewing. You look the types."

Henderson said flatly, "I'll ask you again. Who are you?"

"His name is Simon Larren," said Jouvert calmly. He held out the driving licence from Larren's wallet for Henderson's inspection. "I suppose it's as good a name as any other. There's nothing else here, except cash."

Henderson glanced at the driving licence, but he didn't trouble to take it. He looked down again. "So your name is Larren. But that doesn't mean a thing. Who employs you?"

"He's a detective." Mallory spoke for the first time, his voice still retaining the undercurrent of panic. "He's from Scotland Yard. I told you they were on to me."

"He's not a copper," Henderson silenced the man with the harshness of his voice. "If he was he'd carry a warrant card, and he wouldn't carry a fancy knife. He's not even Special Branch; he's something higher." He glared down at Larren. "What are you?"

"Church of England," Larren said unhelpfully.

Jouvert kicked him calmly but forcefully in the stomach. The sudden agony made Larren's body contract as much as his bonds would allow, and the breath hissed in a strangled gasp through his teeth.

"Have some respect," Jouvert told him. "I do not like comedians."

"That'll do," Henderson said grimly. "It doesn't really matter which department he works for. What matters is how did they get on to Mallory, and how much do they know, but I don't think he's going to tell us. He doesn't look the talking type."

"Everyone is a talking type," Jouvert said softly. "I learned that in the Legion. In Algeria we made even the most stubborn Arabs talk and scream. Some would start as soon as we slit their nostrils; with others it would take a little more time. It is all a matter of technique." He picked up Larren's knife from the table and gently tested the razor-edged blade with his thumb.

Mallory had taken a sudden step backwards, the worried look on his face giving way to a sudden rush of horror as he stared at Jouvert's leathery face. But he was the only one that moved. Andrews was still expressionless, the forgotten cigarette still fixed to his lip. Henderson was merely thoughtful. Larren lay still, but his grey-green eyes never wavered from Jouvert's blue ones.

Jouvert turned finally to Henderson and continued in the same soft tone. "I think I can get him to talk."

"No!" It was Mallory. "I won't stand for torture. It's not going to do us any good. We've got to get away from here, that's the only thing. We've got to get out of —" His flustered voice trailed away as Jouvert turned to stare at him, but it was Henderson who had the final word.

"Shut up, Mallory. I give the orders here." He turned to Jouvert and went on bluntly, "No doubt you could get him to talk, but it's not important. Our job is done and we have only our own escape to worry about. We'll have to leave London now, instead of delaying it for another couple of days." He glanced down at Larren and added: "If his people had any definite line on this place, we'd all be under arrest by now. The fact that he's on his own means that he was simply following Mallory, and provided that he doesn't get back to report then we're still in the clear. We won't need this room again, so we'll destroy it, and him with it."

Mallory's bluff face had paled again. "What do you mean? How are you —?"

"For Christ's sake, shut up!" Henderson's temper exploded into a moment of fury. "This is all your stupid fault, so just stay out of it while we put things right. Andrews, take him with you and use the escape route. Make sure the place isn't under observation as you leave, and then bring the car close up to the door. Jouvert and I will be down as soon as we finish here."

Andrews nodded. "Right, boss. Come on, Mr Mallory, let's get moving."

Mallory hesitated, but Andrews took his shoulder and pushed gently. The greying politician looked deflated and beaten as he allowed himself to be guided out through a second door on the far side of the room. Andrews had produced an automatic as he took the lead, and Mallory's face looked sick as he saw it.

The door closed behind them and Henderson said briefly, "Tape his mouth. He didn't want to talk, so now he'd better stay quiet." He too produced an automatic as he spoke, and he pointed it at the bruise between Larren's eyes. "Don't get any ideas about shouting," he warned. "You'll only be dead that much sooner."

He continued to hold the gun as Jouvert cut two six-inch strips from a wide roll of adhesive tape and pressed them firmly into position across Larren's mouth. Then he put the gun back into his pocket.

"Get the flash-bombs," he said. "We'll leave one in here, and one in the outer room." He looked down at Larren again and explained coldly, "We've been prepared for this for a long time. We knew that ultimately we'd have to abandon this room, and destroy the radio and any other traces of our presence. You've merely caused us to advance our departure by a couple of days."

"What about the woman?" Jouvert spoke from the table that held the radio set, where he was calmly checking the fuses on two identical black canisters. His voice was matter-of-fact and unconcerned, for it was only a technical question.

Henderson left Larren and went into the outer room to examine the still-unconscious body of Little Nancy. He came back and said calmly, "We'll leave her there. She's still out cold, and in any case she knows enough to describe our faces. And as far as I'm concerned that's too much."

Jouvert nodded, and turned away from the table with one of the canisters in his hands. "I'll leave the other one here," he said. "It'll make sure there's nothing left of the radio."

Henderson registered approval, then turned again to Larren. "These things are pretty effective," he said. "They don't make much of a bang, but they throw out plenty of flame. And the panic that will start in that strip club on the floor below will make sure that neither the police nor the fire brigade can get up here in time to do anything to check the fire. So you see, we've considered all the angles."

Jouvert came back into the room, moving swiftly. "I've shortened the fuses," he said crisply. "We've got one minute." He crossed to the canister he had left beside the radio and quickly lit the second fuse.

Henderson threw a last look round the room, then together the two men hurried out of the back door. It slammed behind them and Larren heard the click of a key turning in the lock before their muffled footsteps clattered away. There was nothing then but the hiss of the burning fuses.

For a moment Larren writhed desperately, twisting and jerking on the floor. The tight flex merely cut even deeper into his wrists and thumbs, telling him plainly that Jouvert had trussed him too well to ever escape unaided. Then panic cleared from his mind, and although he knew that his chances of escape were nil, the instinct to survive made him attempt to hang on to life for just a few moments longer.

He wriggled his body closer to the table that stood in the centre of the room, turning his back to it so that his fingers could close on to the nearest leg. With an effort he rolled his body once more, lifting the table leg and twisting his body beneath it. Then he thrust his forehead against the floor, never feeling the pain as he arched his back and toppled the table over on to its side.

It seemed impossible that his sixty seconds were not yet up, and he squirmed his body frantically to get behind the flimsy protection of the tabletop. Then the first flash-bomb exploded in the outer room, a muffled thudding sound that threw a sheet of sudden flame through the open door. Larren made a last scrambling effort and collapsed choking behind his pathetic barrier, and then the second flash-bomb blew itself apart, blasting the transmitter set beside it and spreading fire like a great splashing wave of blazing oil.

In the clubroom below, the first swirls of smoke were barely noticeable as they merged with the heavy pall that lingered in the darkness from the butts of countless cigarettes. A young woman was stripping on the stage, her lithe body moving swiftly and sensually to the thudding drumbeats of the canned jungle music to which she danced. The fast drumming had masked the two muffled thuds from above, and for a moment the silent watching audience was still unaware of the coming danger.

Then a few began to cough, their attention distracted for an instant from the stage, and abruptly there was a yell of alarm as the first of them realised that the atmosphere around them was thickening unnaturally fast. The bloodless young man who waited to check the tickets suddenly dived for the exit and then sent up a shrieking cry of *"FIRE!"* as he saw the first streaks of scarlet flame showing on the upper landing. Without hesitation he plunged down the stairs towards the street.

Behind the tiny stage the young brunette who had been introduced as Madeline — her real name was Annie Goss — sat immersed in a cheap love story as she waited for her turn to appear again. She heard the sudden yells from the clubroom in the same moment that the first drifts of acrid smoke assailed her nostrils and stung her lungs. In sudden horror she stared through a gap in the curtains at the terrifying transformation from silent lechery to struggling tumult as the customers fought to get out, and for a moment she was incapable of movement.

On the stage the dancer was also frozen by fear as her audience went mad with panic. She uttered a piercing scream, grabbing her scattered clothes to her half-naked body as she turned to rush back behind the curtains. The nearer of the customers saw her go, realised that there must be an alternative exit in that direction, and followed her in a mad scramble.

Annie Goss heard the other women shouting to her to run as they fled for safety, but her first thought was not for herself as the first shock passed.

"Nancy!" she cried. "What about Nancy?"

She looked round desperately for help, and in the same moment the first of the stampeding customers were coming over the stage and she was knocked aside and sent sprawling to the floor.

She lay there stunned, cowering from the uproar and wincing from the kicks of trampling feet. The club was filled with smoke and the sound of choking almost drowned the screams of fear. There was complete pandemonium around her as men used fists and feet to battle their way to the two exits, and then the two spotlights that covered the stage dimmed abruptly and darkness added to the crazed confusion.

Swiftly, despite the panic, the club began to empty, its struggling clientele draining away down the two escape routes. Annie Goss pulled herself to her feet again, coughing and spluttering as the smoke filled her mouth. She was sick with fear, but still she thought of Nancy. She knew that Nancy must still be on the floor above.

She stumbled into the main clubroom and across to the main exit, getting caught up with the last desperate handful of customers trying to get out. She was almost carried down the stairs towards the street, but she twisted frantically away from the mob and ran up towards the next landing. The door above was blazing, but her mind was gripped with one thought, drawn by a tie that eclipsed even the fear of death, and she crashed her shoulder against the burning door and forced her way in.

She cowered behind her own arm as the wall of blazing flame seemed to fling itself around her, and her blouse was burning as she ran through and into the room. She saw the slack form of Little Nancy sprawled on her back on the bed and grabbed her frantically by the shoulders.

"Nance! Nance, for God's sake!"

She screamed the words above the roar of the fire, but the woman's blonde head simply rolled to one side. Annie tried to lift her up hut failed. Her reason was going now and she was crazed by fear, she couldn't breathe and she knew that she was going to die with Nancy. Then she saw the second open door.

She left Nancy and pushed through into the second blazing room, hoping for a window from which she could scream for help. There was none, and she fell sobbing to her knees.

That was when she saw Simon Larren. The table that had shielded him from the actual blast of the flash-bomb was now blazing merrily, and he had wriggled his body as far away as possible from the flames. He was still conscious, although only just, and he barely believed in the sudden appearance of the agonised girl in the burning blouse.

As he watched Annie Goss twisted and tore the garment from her back, sobbing as it came away from her raw shoulders. Pain filled her body, but still she had the instinct to survive, and she recognised that only Larren could help her. There was no real thought in her mind as her fingers picked at the flex binding his wrists, and she broke most of her nails before realising that it was hopeless. In desperation she did the only thing that she could and tore the tape from his mouth.

Larren gasped at the smoke-laden air, hanging on weakly to his fading grip on life.

"Pliers," he said, and wasn't sure whether his hoarse croak had sounded above the hideous crackle of the flames. "They were on the table. They fell off to the floor."

Perhaps she heard him and perhaps she didn't, but her searching eyes saw the pliers that Jouvert had used lying a yard away and she scrambled to reach them. She worked clumsily, but the pliers were sharp and it took only a few seconds to cut him free.

Larren called upon the last reservoirs of his strength, making the supreme effort to stay above the black haze that swamped his bursting brain. He reached his feet and pulled up the girl beside him. The far door was afire and he kicked it open, splintering it away from the hinges. The girl pushed away from him.

"Nancy," she begged weakly. "Get Nancy for me, *please*!"

Larren remembered the woman he had knocked unconscious; he returned and humped her over one shoulder, stumbling blindly as he rejoined Annie Goss. He hooked one arm round the younger woman's waist, careless of her burned flesh, and together they groped their way along the smoke-filled passageway that was Henderson's escape route. Behind them there was a final roar as the roof of the building thundered inwards, and a blast of flame drove them on.

Larren could no longer breathe when they found a descending staircase, and Annie was helpless beside him. His senses reeled away and he collapsed, tumbling face first down the stairs and dragging the two women with him. They sprawled out into a back street and lay still on the pavement, three corpses nearer to death than life. Above them sparks cascaded up to the night sky, and an approaching fire engine violently clanged its bell.

CHAPTER 5: VAGUE CLUES

Larren recovered consciousness for the second time as he was being lifted on to a stretcher, and he began to struggle feebly. On the far pavement a jostling crowd had already gathered and were being held back by a handful of policemen. Both the ambulance and the fire brigade had arrived and the men who manned them were efficiently taking control. Helmeted firemen spun great rolls of grey-white hose along the road as their fire-escape ladders strained up into the smoke and flame-filled sky, while the ambulance teams were already carrying away the two women Larren had brought out of the burning strip club.

"Steady, old chap. Take it easy now."

The ambulance attendant spoke quietly but firmly, pressing down on Larren's shoulder as the two stretcher-bearers lifted him off the ground. Larren tried to sit up, but the world was a crazy roaring haze that circled dizzily around him and his body was racked by a fit of helpless coughing. His mouth worked weakly as he sucked in air, fighting the agony of his pain-filled lungs. His eyes smarted as though the inside of his eyelids were faced with red-hot sandpaper, and the tears streamed past them as he tried to see.

"Take it easy now," the white-coated man repeated. "It's going to be all right."

Larren twisted away from the restraining hand and pushed back the grey blanket that covered him. The stretcher rocked and was almost dropped as he succeeded in his second attempt to sit up. The leading stretcher bearer twisted his head, shouting angrily, but Larren had already grabbed the lapels of that nearest white coat and was pulling himself to his feet. For a moment he still couldn't speak, and then he forced the words out.

"This — this is important." His mouth seemed as raw as his lungs and every croaking syllable hurt abominably, but he managed to go on. "Must telephone — important."

"It'll keep. Nothing's that important."

The man was curt and angry now, and he wrenched hard at Larren's wrists to disentangle the clutching fingers. Larren hung on stubbornly, trying to rally his strength, and then a young policeman moved wearily towards the scene.

"What's up with this one?" His tone reflected a low opinion of strip club customers, and Larren felt a rush of despair. The policeman's hand gripped firmly at his shoulder. "Come on, sir. Get back on the stretcher."

Larren looked at the black-gloved hand on his shoulder, then into the hard eyes beneath the peaked cap. He realised then that this was no constable on the beat, and for the first time saw the black crime car parked a few yards away. Desperately he tried again.

"Listen to me. The man you want in connection with the P.M.'s killing left that club barely ten minutes ago." It took a supreme effort to keep his voice clear and convincing, but he completed another sentence. "He left in a car with three other men."

The hard eyes stared back at him. "Are you sure about this, sir?"

"Blast you," Larren said savagely. "Contact your information room. Get them to call Whitehall 0-1-0. Ask —" His lungs twisted with another wave of coughing, and when it subsided he finished weakly, "Ask for extension double-0."

The policeman stared for another second, then made up his mind. "Bring him over to the car," he told the ambulance attendant.

The attendant hesitated, but the policeman was already hurrying across to the crime car, and after a moment he gave Larren some more solid support and helped him to follow. By the time they got there the policeman was already speaking briskly into a radio telephone. He passed on what Larren had told him, and finished with a request for the Whitehall number. There was a long minute of waiting, and then he turned and handed the telephone to Larren. A flat, toneless voice issued out of the earpiece.

"Caller, identify yourself, please."

Larren drew a deep breath. "This is Watchdog M. to Watchdog Master. Mallory has just made contact with a man who fits the description we issued in connection with the P.M.'s killing. I'm speaking from outside the Sultry Strip Club in the Soho area. They left here less than fifteen minutes ago in a car in company with two other men. I don't know the make of the car, or where they're heading, but I think they're leaving the city and road blocks might stop them."

He went on to describe Andrews and Henderson, and added brief details of what had happened. The police car crew and the ambulance attendant listened in silence, and Larren knew that he had compromised the Watchdog call signs and the telephone number, but that was just too bad and they would simply have to be changed. This information had to go through, even though he doubted whether they could act on it in time to achieve any results.

He finally determined the name of the hospital to which he and the two women were being taken and passed it on before returning the telephone to the waiting car crew. There was nothing more that he could do now, and he felt suddenly sick. He turned away and was helped across to the ambulance that was still waiting for him.

Little Nancy lay motionless on the stretcher bed against the left side wall, covered with a blanket and still unconscious, while the younger woman lay face down on the stretcher opposite. Her face was twisted against the agony of her badly burned back and shoulders despite the morphia that had already been given to her. Her eyes opened as Larren was helped in, and he knelt for a moment beside her.

He said quietly, "That was a very brave thing you did, young lady." Then he paused awkwardly, wondering, before asking, "But what made you do it?"

She made an effort to blink away the tears in her eyes and her mouth trembled uncontrollably before she could answer. "I did it for Nance." She recognised the signs of puzzlement that lingered in his eyes and her face filled with grief. She said bitterly, "I don't suppose she means much in your book. Just a dirty old whore. But she's my sister — she's all I've got." And then her face turned away and she was crying wretchedly.

Larren said nothing, watching silently in a moment of rare compassion. And then he thought grimly that this was perhaps the only angle Henderson had failed to consider.

Despite Larren's protests, he was detained in hospital for the rest of the night and most of the following day. On police instructions he was given a private room, and immediately after he arrived Adrian Cleyton appeared. The slim man listened intently as Larren repeated his story, then assured him that the hunt was being intensified for Mallory and his three companions. It was a short visit, and after Cleyton had left Larren was given a sedative that put him out for the next fourteen hours.

When he awoke he argued again with his doctors, and finally, late on the Sunday afternoon they allowed him to leave. He was somewhat shaky and his chest was still sore, but fortunately his nervous system was accustomed to bouts of violence and he suffered no reactions from shock. He had painful burns on his hands and face, but the biggest damage was to his suit, which had smouldered beyond recognition. He made a rash promise to attend the hospital's outpatients' department daily for treatment, then telephoned the caretaker's wife at Rushlake Terrace and persuaded her to bring him a decent set of clothes from the wardrobe in his flat.

At six o'clock that evening he reported to Whitehall. Smith received him in the book-lined office from which he operated and gave him an appraising look. "You should have stayed in bed, Larren. You look a mess."

Larren shrugged. "I feel a mess. But it occurs to me that as I'm the only man who has actually met Henry Mallory's little playmates, I might possibly be of some use."

Smith smiled, and looked for a moment like a fond uncle. He was a short, paunchy little man who habitually favoured a bowler hat and a pinstriped suit, a chameleon who merged unseen into his chosen background of all the unidentifiable little men who filled the city's offices in their thousands. Outside of this office and its equivalent top-level rooms in Whitehall, no one would ever take a second look at Smith, for the real man lay behind the grey eyes and the rest was just a faceless mask.

"Perhaps you're right," he said. "You seem to have crashed your way right into the heart of this job, so I might as well bring you up to date. After your call came through last night I cleared you through our liaison with Special Branch at the

Yard. Their information room acted on your advice and the Metropolitan Police blocked all roads out of the city. However, that took time, and unless your friends are still in London then they've slipped through the net. It would have helped of course if you could have told them what kind of car they were looking for."

"No doubt it would have helped if I had arrested them all on the spot," Larren observed wryly. "But it didn't work out that way."

"No rebuke intended." Smith smiled again, and that was as near as he would get to a word of praise. "But we've got them on the run, and we've got descriptions of the men we want. And we've built up a pretty good picture of what was going on at the strip club, thanks to Nancy Goss, the prostitute you pulled out of the fire." He smiled a third time, and Larren thought that he was unusually full of smiles. "Of course, we didn't tell her that it was one of our men who laid her out in the first place, but we did impress upon her that Henderson and Jouvert had deliberately left her there to die. She gave us their names after that, and everything else she knew.

"There were half a dozen others who attended meetings above the strip club, and although they're undoubtedly small fry we've got her to describe them as well as she can remember. These meetings apparently took place about once a fortnight during the three months previous to the P.M.'s death. There were no secret passwords or anything like that, and either Henderson or Andrews would simply keep watch through the peephole when their own visitors were expected and then come forward to let them in.

"The last of these meetings took place ten days before the P.M. was assassinated, and three days before the assassination Henderson moved in permanently. The man Andrews was there all the time as caretaker and radio operator. It was about the same time that Jouvert made his first appearance, together with another man named Skoda, who was obviously the man we found dead after he had fired the fatal shot at Sir Howard Davies." Smith paused for a moment, his pudgy face serious, and Larren realised that the little man had used up his day's quota of smiles. "That was all Nancy Goss could tell us. The owner of the strip club has disappeared as you might expect, and Scotland Yard are trying to trace him now. It seems that Henderson and his two lieutenants used only the back entrance to that room behind Nancy's, so the strippers below and the doormen had no idea of what was really going on."

Larren was silent for a moment, then asked, "How is the younger girl?"

"Annie Goss? She's in a bad way. She suffered worse burns that either you or her sister when she forced her way into Nancy's room. She'll most certainly never do a strip tease dance again. Men don't pay to see scarred flesh." He became briefly human and said softly, "You were very lucky, Larren. Courage flares in some strange places."

Larren nodded, feeling almost humble, something he had never experienced before. "Were there no fresh leads? Nothing else to go on?"

"Nothing definite," Smith said quietly. "But there were some vague pointers from Nancy Goss. One, she had caught some scraps of conversation from the men who passed through her room, and she believed that they called themselves the A.F.P., although what those three letters might stand for she had no idea. And two, she had once heard Henderson complain that it had taken him over three hours to drive up to London, and on another occasion he had mentioned a traffic jam at Cheltenham, which seems to place his starting point somewhere in Gloucestershire. We've passed that information on to the chief constable of the area, and he's co-operating with a county-wide search. Every local copper and special constable in that part of the country has been alerted to watch any isolated houses or hotels where a group of strangers could hide up." He paused wryly, and concluded, "When the odds are against us we still rely upon the good old copper on the beat to pull us out of a mess."

Larren looked up and said slowly, "If Gloucestershire *is* a possibility, then perhaps I should get down there. They'll need someone to make a positive identification if they do get a line on Henderson and his friends."

"You mean that you want to be in at the kill." Smith returned his gaze coldly as he spoke. Then he nodded dubiously. "But perhaps you're right. I should leave it to Special Branch and the local police, but in the circumstances, and with a killer like Jouvert involved, I'd rather that you were on hand to deal with him. But remember that I want him alive."

CHAPTER 6: IN SILENCE AND IN DARKNESS

Larren drove his white MG across country later that Sunday night, and by midnight he was in Gloucester. Smith had smoothed the way for him and he was expected, and immediately on his arrival he made himself known to a Chief Superintendent Parker, who was the senior of the two Special Branch men leading the hunt with the county police force. Larren again repeated everything he knew about the four men who had escaped from the Sultry Strip for the first-hand benefit of Parker and his colleagues, but there was nothing that they could tell him in return. They were feverishly sifting reports and checking false alarms from all parts of the county, but so far they had made no definite progress that would help to pinpoint their search. They still had nothing more than the vague clues given by Nancy Goss on which to base their operations, and, as Parker gloomily observed, the fact that Henderson had once made a trip through Cheltenham to London didn't necessarily mean that he had his bolt hole in the area. He might have been simply visiting a friend. Larren appreciated the problems, but there was nothing that he could do at this stage except stand by and hope that the search would eventually bear fruit.

He stood by for the next two frustrating days, staying at a hotel close to the central police station that Parker had made his battle headquarters. The waiting galled him, but at least it gave him time to recover more fully from his ordeal by fire. He slept as much as impatience would allow, for he knew the value of storing sleep when there was nothing else to be done, and when events were likely to explode in the near future, but he was wide awake when the mass hunt at last showed results.

A telephone call brought him hurrying to the police station, where Parker was in conference with his Special Branch assistant, a detective inspector named Rowlands, and a ring of senior officers of the county C.I.D. Parker looked up, shifting his sixteen-stone bulk in his chair as Larren was shown into the room where they were all gathered. His square-jawed face showed a brief smile of satisfaction as he said, "I think we may have found them, Larren."

He stood up and indicated a large-scale map of the county that hung upon the wall. "We've had a report from a little place called Bowington. It's here, just inside the county boundary. It seems that there's a large country house about a mile or so from the village; it's set in a couple of acres of private grounds and goes under the name of Larkspurs. It stood empty for about a year after the death of the previous owner, but six months ago it was sold. The new owners only seem to appear there on odd occasions, and nobody seems to know much about them, which was what first aroused the interest of one of the local constables when he was told to keep an eye open for anything suspicious. Now he's turned in a report that the residents of a nearby cottage heard a car draw up at Larkspurs in the early hours of Sunday morning, and that the house is now occupied."

Larren said grimly, "It sounds promising."

Parker smiled again. "It gets better. A local milkman called there this morning, just a polite visit, hoping to add another call to his rounds. He was told rather bluntly that they wouldn't be wanting any regular deliveries, and afterwards he mentioned it to our constable. The description he gave of the man who answered the door could fit your description of Andrews." He came away from the map and concluded, "Inspector Rowlands and I are going down to Bowington now, and Inspector Gracey will accompany us to represent County C.I.D. We'll need you with us, Larren, to make a positive identification."

Gracey, a tall, severe man, added dubiously, "I've had permission from the Home Office to issue arms to my senior men, but I'm not sure whether that should include you. You're not exactly under my command."

Larren smiled and opened his jacket to reveal the Smith & Wesson .38 that fitted the shoulder holster beneath his left arm. "Don't worry about it, Inspector," he said. "My own department makes sure that I'm properly equipped."

Gracey still looked uncertain, but then Parker smiled and said, "We'll assume that he has got a licence. Right now the cars are waiting."

An hour later Simon Larren stood by the bonnet of a black police car on a narrow country road only half a mile from the private driveway that led to Larkspurs. Parker, Rowlands and Gracey were still with him, but now they were joined by the station inspector from Bowington. They had held a final briefing in the cramped village police station, and now they waited while the station sergeant and his two constables led two separate parties of picked policemen to surround the house.

The night was dark, moonless, and showing only a few stars. The countryside around them was thickly wooded, and Larren could imagine the grim faces of the policemen as they threaded their way through the trees to throw their cordon around the house. It was the kind of night that would always stir his blood, for these were the conditions in which he best loved to operate. There was no better cover than the hours of darkness.

In the past hour the Gloucestershire C.I.D. had tracked down the house agent who had handled the sale of Larkspurs six months previously, and his description of the buyer had fitted perfectly with Henderson. This fact had been relayed to Bowington, and now both Larren and Parker were convinced that they were closing in on the men they sought. The local men had watched Larkspurs since the place was first brought to their attention, and they were able to swear that no one had left the house or grounds.

Fifteen minutes passed, then Parker looked up from his wristwatch and said calmly, "They should be in position now. It's time we approached the house."

They returned to the small convoy of police cars that lined the road, and the convoy drove quietly forward. They were soon passing a shoulder-high wall which enclosed the wooded grounds and the house, and then the entrance to the driveway showed up in the gloom ahead, for none of the cars was showing lights. The cars stopped and the small force of men scrambled swiftly out.

There were seven of them: Larren, the two Special Branch men, the Bowington inspector, and Gracey and two of his most efficient detective sergeants. The heavy iron gates between the two square pillars flanking the driveway were closed but not locked, and they pushed them open and walked briskly up the gravel drive. On either side the trees stood hushed and silent, and there was no wind. The only sound was the sharp scuff of their feet through the chips of gravel.

The path curved to the left, and once they turned the slight bend they saw the house a hundred yards ahead. It was a large, square building, and any distinctive character it might have had was hidden in its shadows. It could have been Georgian, Tudor or Elizabethan, but as they saw it now it was no more than a black mass in the darkness, and even the slant of roofs and chimneys was barely distinguishable. The only signs of life came from two upper windows, where lights showed faintly behind thick drawn curtains. They were like square, off-set eyes, peering from one side of a hidden face.

There was no word among the approaching party, but their steps quickened now that they were in view of the house. The two sergeants produced heavy flashlights, but as yet they did not attempt to use them. There was no sign of the men forming the cordon, whom they knew must be waiting round the sides and at the back of the building.

They reached the front door and waited in silence while Parker rang the bell. Larren stood just behind the superintendent's shoulder and felt the tension that had affected them all, for no one knew what the next few minutes might provide. Larren himself did not approve of this bold frontal approach, but it was Parker's show and Larren had no real say in the matter. Technically he was only here to identify the quarry.

There was silence after the chiming echoes of the bell died away, and Parker reached out to stab the button a second time. He stopped as they heard footsteps inside, and there was a sharp click of a light being switched on. A moment later the door was pulled cautiously open.

It was Andrews. Larren saw the inevitable cigarette drooping from the man's lip, but even more important, a squat black automatic drooping from his right hand. The cigarette dropped as his jaw slackened, but the automatic lifted sharply up.

"Coppers!"

Andrews yelled the warning frantically as Larren's shoulder crashed the door fully open. The gun in his hand barked once, the spitting report drowning the gasping cry of agony as one of the party was hit. Then Larren's fingers closed on the gun wrist, twisting and swinging Andrews fully round. The automatic clattered to the floor as Andrews yelled, and then the stiffened fingers of Larren's hand thrust savagely into his kidneys and doubled him up into Parker's arms.

Larren's hand was already dipping inside his jacket, freeing the Smith & Wesson as he dashed forward. Behind him Rowlands, the second Special Branch man, was slithering to the floor with both hands clutching the bullet wound in his stomach, paying the policeman's price for waiting to be shot at first before producing his specially issued gun. But Larren had no policeman's scruples.

The front door opened on to a spacious reception room with doors on either side, but there was a wide staircase leading up to a landing at the far end, and remembering the lights that they had seen from outside Larren guessed that Andrews's companions were up above. Two tough-looking men rushed him as he reached the foot of the staircase, but they were strangers and were unarmed. Larren bowled one aside with his gun-laden fist and the other turned abruptly back as he saw the massive bulk of Parker charging up in support.

There was a shout from Gracey and one of the detective sergeants dived after the defector. The second sergeant held the still-crippled Andrews in a vicious arm lock, while Gracey ran to join Parker. Simon Larren went up the stairs three at a time as the sandy-haired figure of Henderson burst into view on the landing.

Henderson fired blindly and Larren ducked sideways as a bullet sent splinters flying from the handrail beside his head.

He missed his step and tumbled to his knees as Henderson fired again. Larren aimed the Smith & Wesson in the hope of hitting the man in the legs and bringing him down, but Henderson retreated too fast into a doorway behind him.

Larren crouched on the stairs, hesitant of making a suicide rush up to the landing. Behind him Parker bellowed out to Henderson to give himself up, while Gracey shrilly blew his whistle to signal the cordon outside to close.

There was no reply from Henderson, and no sign of Jouvert or Mallory. Larren steeled himself to move, then thrust himself forward in a fast zigzagging run up the stairs. He fired twice as he went, shooting through the open door through which Henderson had vanished. The shots were meant to hold Henderson back while he gained the landing, but they were a waste of ammunition because Henderson was no longer there. Larren realised that when the room ahead blew up with a sheet of flame and the blast knocked him back down the staircase.

Larren lay against the handrail, winded by his fall, and recognised the effects of another of the flash-bombs that had been used to destroy the room above the Sultry Strip. *Not again,* he thought bitterly; but there was no time for regrets. The stairs shook beneath him as Parker thundered past, and Gracey was close on his heels. The two policemen had drawn their revolvers now, and their faces showed that they felt justified to use them.

Larren pulled himself up and stumbled after them, and all three milled on the landing, flinching from the heat that beat at them from the open doorway. There was no sign of Henderson in the flame-filled room, and they spread out on the landing, Larren moving right, and Parker and Gracey moving left.

Larren tried the first door he came to, kicking it open and barging straight in. The room was empty, but there was another door beyond, and knowing that Henderson must have escaped to the back of the house Larren carried on through. He was on his own now, but that hardly mattered.

He found himself in a narrow corridor and ran left until he found a main right-angle turning. There was smoke behind him, and he knew that he had bypassed the burning room. Henderson must be ahead.

All was in darkness now and he pulled a flashlight from his pocket as he ran. The torch showed the corridor ending at the top of a descending stairway and he stopped and shone the beam down from the open landing. It picked out the thick-set figure of Henderson at the bottom of the staircase, and again Henderson turned to fire. The bullet went wild as an outside door crashed inwards behind him and more flashlights fixed him against the wall. For a moment he stood there like a performer trapped on a makeshift stage, and then a main light was switched on to show up the scene below. A burly sergeant and two constables, part of the outside cordon, had broken in through the back door in answer to Gracey's whistle, and now they formed a solid wedge to block Henderson's retreat. The fugitive turned his gaze desperately upwards, and in the same moment more lights flashed on behind the waiting figure of Larren as Parker and Gracey hurried up behind him.

Henderson fired two more wild shots, one at Larren and one at the men below him. Then, as they all fell back, he fumbled in his pocket and then clapped a hand to his mouth.

Larren saw the fleeting expression of agony that crossed Henderson's face as his throat worked in a final convulsive gulp, and regardless of the other's gun he hurled himself down the stairs. He knocked Henderson flying and they tumbled to ground level where the three uniformed men rushed to assist him, but by then Henderson was already choking on his last few breaths.

Larren stood up, panting slightly as Parker and Gracey came slowly down the stairs. Henderson lay still at his feet.

"Cyanide?" Parker asked grimly.

Larren nodded. "That, or something as deadly." He looked up. "Any sign of the other two?"

Parker shook his head. "Not yet, but some of the men who cordoned the house are searching it now, and they're trying to put that fire out. It looks as though Henderson had another radio transmitter in that room which he wanted to destroy."

Larren pulled a sour face, and in that moment they heard a faint shout from outside, followed almost instantaneously by the ringing, high-powered crack of a rifle. Larren swore and dived for the back door, and the others surged behind him.

He ran round the side of the house towards the sound, and then saw a handful of uniformed men fanning out and moving away from the house. From behind him Gracey shouted and one of the men turned to answer.

"There's one of them got away, sir. He slipped through one of the side windows and made a run for the woods. Some of the chaps still in the cordon headed him off to the right and he took a shot at one of them. He's got a rifle."

"Jouvert," Larren said flatly. "I was afraid of this."

The rifle sounded again, cracking sharply in the darkness to their right, and as if to echo Larren's forebodings there was a sharp cry of pain as the target was hit. Larren carried on running, cutting through the shouting and confusion, then one voice bellowed above the rest: "He's in the conservatory!"

Larren recognised the shout of the Bowington station sergeant, and then he heard Parker yelling in turn, "Spread out around him. But for God's sake don't get too close."

A moment later the solid figure of the sergeant loomed up out of the darkness, and Larren checked himself just in time to avoid a collision. Behind him grass and twigs crackled under the running feet of Parker and Gracey as they came to join him. The sergeant said breathlessly, "The conservatory's that way, sir. In the middle of that bit of open land. I think he was crossing the open stretch when he realised that we had more men on the other side. He's pretty well surrounded, but I don't know how we're going to flush him out."

Gracey was breathing harshly, and his face was strained in the gloom. "We could rush him," he said. "Enough of us are armed."

"With revolvers," Parker reminded him. "That man's got a rifle."

"Then how do we get him out?" Gracey demanded.

Parker had no answer, but Larren said grimly, "You won't. I will. Keep your men well back out of harm's way, but make sure you maintain the cordon. Spread out the senior men with the arms to make sure he doesn't break through. I'll go after Jouvert alone."

Gracey stared at him doubtfully. "This isn't a one-man job."

"It is now," Larren contradicted him. "If you try to close the circle around that conservatory then you'll lose some more good coppers. Jouvert's an expert. He'll pick them off like ducks in a shooting gallery. But I'm something of an expert too. I've had the right kind of training. I stand a better chance of getting close to him than anyone else."

There was an empty silence, then Parker said, “He’s right, Gracey. I know a little about his department. It’s our responsibility, but I think we should let him try.”

Gracey drew a breath and nodded. “All right. Sergeant, make your way quietly round the circle and tell the men to stay well back. We don’t want any more of them killed.” He waited until the man had nodded and moved off into the darkness, then he said, “Is there anything else that we can do to help?”

Larren shook his head. “I’ll either make it or I won’t. If anyone comes with me it only doubles the chances that Jouvert will hear us before we get close enough to do any good.”

Gracey still looked worried. “Good luck,” he said.

Larren smiled and glanced upwards to the unrelieved blackness of the sky. Not even a star was visible, and somehow he knew that this was his element. He could move in silence, and he had the cover of total darkness, and he knew that it was enough. He barely needed any luck.

CHAPTER 7: TRAIL TO TANGIER

It took Larren over half an hour to get within striking distance of the small conservatory, for although the night and an expanse of low bushes gave him plenty of cover he was in no hurry. The air was wholly silent now, but poignant with a sense of expectancy. The outer ring of policemen had been warned to do nothing that might reveal their positions and perhaps attract a shot, and waited like frozen shadows in the surrounding woods. To the left the dark hulk of Larkspurs brooded, again an indistinctive mass against the vaguely lesser darkness of the sky. The fire inside had been brought under control and the lights had been switched off to give Larren the background he needed.

He could distinguish the conservatory now; it was some twenty yards ahead of him as he lay motionless against a clump of shrubs. There was no sound from inside, and there had been no sound for the past twenty minutes. Then there had been the sharp smashing of glass, presumably as Jouvert had knocked firing holes through the windows with the butt of his rifle.

Larren wondered how Jouvert was feeling, whether the waiting was fraying at the man's nerves. The assassin must be crouching there in his cramped and final refuge, listening and wondering. Able to cover practically all directions through the mainly glass walls, but not knowing until the last moment from where the attack might come. The thought made Larren smile faintly, even though the odds were still against him.

For another five minutes Larren lay perfectly still, gradually determining the construction of the building he could only vaguely see. The side walls were solid up to about three feet, and then there were full-width windows up to roof level. The end walls looked solid, but he guessed that there would be a smaller window at the back. The roof was tiled, but there was a row of three raised skylights running the full length. Twice his keen ears picked up movements from inside, not enough to mark Jouvert's position, but enough to tell him that Jouvert was shifting about, and consequently that the man was worried. The transformation to utter silence after the hectic shouting and activity of thirty minutes ago must have got him rattled. He would have anticipated that they would rush his position long before this, but now he would not know what to expect.

Gingerly, like a wary cobra slithering low through the grass, Larren began to circle round to the back end of the building ahead. He moved an inch at a time, patient and unhurried, his fingers lightly probing the earth in front of him and carefully removing any twigs that could snap or leaves that could crackle. He had all the time in the world. All the time between life and death.

His approach was soundless, and when at last he lay close against the end wall of the conservatory he knew that Jouvert had not an inkling that he was there. With the same slow care he straightened his body and stood with his back pressed to the wall, his head close to the small back window.

For the first time he hesitated. The Smith & Wesson .38 was snug in its holster beneath his armpit, and the knife he favoured was still fitted into the hidden sheath inside his jacket. But Smith had said that he wanted Jouvert alive, and now that

Henderson was dead, the assassin would be even more important. Reluctantly, Larren left both weapons in their place.

For a brief moment longer he enjoyed the protective shield of almost total darkness, waiting and listening, and then he turned and reached up to grip the edge of the roof above him. He heard Jouvert shuffle inside as he pulled gently, then more strongly to ensure that the tiles would take the strain, then heaved himself up.

His clothes rustled and the toe of his shoe scratched against the wall as he balanced on his arms with the edge of the roof cutting into the lower half of his stomach. He ignored silence then, thrusting himself upright and throwing up both arms to protect his face as he jumped squarely on to the centre of the closed glass skylights.

He landed in an explosion of flying glass and lunged towards the sound of Jouvert's startled cry. The barrel of the rifle smacked against his shoulder as Jouvert swung it to meet him in the Stygian blackness, and the crack of the bullet slammed against his ear as their bodies collided. More glass shattered as the bullet tore its way outside into the night, and Jouvert desperately triggered off a second shot as they went down together to the floor. A host of unseen seed trays and plant pots clattered down with them, and they struggled wildly in the wreckage. The rifle was torn away from Jouvert's hand, and he screamed as his trapped index finger was broken in the trigger guard.

Outside, police whistles shrilled as the cordon broke forward, and blind frenzy gave Jouvert a tigerish strength. Larren was taller than the Frenchman and a little heavier, but it was all that he could do to hold his own as they fought like wildcats. More pots and seed boxes crashed around them as they rolled furiously through a mess of crushed plants, soil and broken pottery and glass. For a moment they broke apart, and Jouvert's boot lashed out to catch Larren on the shoulder and send him spinning. The Frenchman was on his feet a second later and Larren heard him dive for the door. Frantically Larren pushed himself up and fell forwards in a flying tackle that ended with his arms wrapped around Jouvert's knees. Jouvert cursed as he was brought down again, twisting around and kicking out with both feet. Larren lost his grip and stopped one flailing boot with his jaw. He slumped back groggily as Jouvert writhed away, and then abruptly Jouvert gave a gurgling cry. The Frenchman gagged helplessly, as though an unseen hand was throttling the life out of him, and then he was still.

A minute later the door was kicked open and a battery of flashlights lit up the scene. Larren crouched on one knee in the shambles that was all that was left of the conservatory. He was panting weakly and bleeding from a scattering of minor cuts that he had collected from the sea of broken glass. Before him lay Jouvert. The assassin sprawled on his back and there was a knot of pain across the dead, leathery face. His throat was speared by a long sliver of jagged glass that was still attached to part of the broken frame from the skylight.

Larren rose shakily to his feet, and Gracey emerged from behind the blaze of lights to help him. The big bulk that was Parker followed and stooped over the dead man.

"Blast and damn it," the Special Branch man said bitterly. "Of all the lousy luck."

"We've still got Andrews," Gracey said. "At least that's one alive."

"He might talk, but he won't know much." Larren had recovered a little and no longer needed any help. He looked down at Parker and added, "But we've only accounted for three of them. What happened to Henry Mallory?"

"There was no sign of him," Parker said. "No sign whatsoever."

It was shortly after dawn when Larren again confronted Smith at Whitehall. The paunchy little man looked as prim and orderly as ever, and there was nothing about him to suggest that he had been hastily recalled to the office. He looked up from his desk as Larren came in, offering no greeting but saying simply, "I should have known that if I sent you then Jouvert would end up dead."

"It was an accident," Larren said wearily. "I did my best."

"Your best invariably results in accidents — fatal ones for other people. Sit down."

Larren sat down, facing him across the desk, and waited.

Smith stabbed a podgy finger at a typed report lying on the blotter in front of him. "This has just come in from Scotland Yard. Parker sent the rifle Jouvert used to the Yard laboratory and they've just completed a rush ballistics test. The markings on the test bullet they fired match up perfectly with the bullet they dug out of Skoda's head, so there's no doubt that Jouvert was the second assassin."

"So that finishes the case?" Larren phrased it as a question rather than a statement, sensing that it was not so.

"Not quite." Smith paused for a moment and then went on. "There are things that I'm not happy about. On the face of it we've caught up with the P.M.'s killers, but one thing we haven't found is a motive. Only a crank kills on impulse or in anger, but these people were a well-organised group. Why did they do it? There was no political motive, for the country is still being governed under Sir Howard's deputy premier in exactly the same way as it was before. They haven't even forced a general election. And there was no direct financial gain for anybody. So, what was the motive?"

Larren said nothing. It was an aspect he had not considered before, and he had no answers.

Smith stood up suddenly, a sure sign that he was worried, and walked round the desk to stand on one side of the room. Larren had to twist in his chair to face him as the little man continued.

"These are the facts: Jouvert and Skoda were paid assassins. They were paid to assassinate Sir Howard Davies by a mysterious group that we know vaguely by the initials A.F.P. There were long range radio transmitters both at Larkspurs in Gloucestershire and at the Sultry Strip, which means that they were in contact with foreign stations. In fact, it's highly probable that they were directed by those foreign stations. Why? What's behind it all?" He turned and rested both hands on the edge of the desk, leaning forwards. "There is something behind it, Larren. Something even bigger than the death of the Prime Minister. I can sense it."

Larren said slowly, "Will Andrews talk?"

"He might if I could give him to someone like you. But he's in police hands. Sure, Parker will grill him, he might even get rough considering that Chief Inspector Rowlands died from that bullet in the stomach. But Parker and his colleagues are still policemen, they'll stick to the letter of the law. No physical ill-treatment of prisoners, even if they are murderers." He dismissed the prospect of Andrews talking and asked abruptly, "What do you think happened to Henry Mallory?"

Larren reflected a moment. "I think they probably murdered him. He was panicking and his usefulness was over. It would be the logical thing for them to do."

Smith frowned. "That's true. But there was no trace of him at Larkspurs, and although Gloucestershire C.I.D. are still searching the surrounding woods with dogs, they have so far failed to find a body. I think that Mallory might be still alive."

"Where?"

Smith gave him a straight look. "In Morocco. You told me yourself that when you first recovered consciousness in the strip club they were promising to arrange his escape."

"That's true," Larren admitted. "But Henderson was simply trying to keep him quiet. I don't think he meant it."

"I'm not so sure," Smith retorted. "You must remember that Henderson could not foresee that he would be so swiftly traced to Larkspurs. He must have believed that he had got clean away from London and that his troubles were over, and I don't think that he would have taken the risk of murdering Mallory in England. Murder means a body to get rid of, bloodstains, and other complications. It's more likely that if they were in a position to smuggle Mallory out of the country to Morocco then they would have done so. After all, they could always kill him later if need be, in Tangier or somewhere where a stray corpse would create less fuss."

"It's possible," Larren said slowly. "We know from the radio transmitters that they had contacts abroad, and there are one or two pointers to North Africa. Jouvert once mentioned Algeria and the Legion, so it's a certainty that he served out there before the French Foreign Legion was disbanded. But one fact doesn't fit. If they were in a position to get Mallory to Morocco, then why didn't they all go with him?"

"Perhaps their job in England was not quite finished." Smith paused and then added, "But I don't think that was it. They probably chose to lie low until the heat had cooled. You must remember that that identikit sketch of Jouvert was on the front page of every paper in the U.K., not to mention ninety per cent of the papers in Europe. Mallory could get through unnoticed where Jouvert would be instantly recognised."

Larren waited as Smith returned to his seat behind the desk, a sure sign that he was about to dispense some definite orders, then he said quietly, "So what happens now?"

"The investigation goes on. Special Branch will continue to try and get something out of Andrews, and they'll keep on digging into the background of Henderson and Jouvert. We, in our own more subtle ways, will be working to the same end." Smith eyed him keenly and then finished, "But I think we can manage without you, Larren. I can spare you for the long shot. You'll take the noon plane to Tangier, and you'll work with our agent there. If Henry Mallory was spirited away to Morocco, then Tangier is the most likely place for him to have gone to earth. Your job is to dig him out."

It was raining as Simon Larren left Whitehall, but in Switzerland the skies were a vivid blue and the only clouds were as purely white as the high-peaked Alps that gleamed in snowy splendour beneath the morning sunshine. The placid waters of Lake Zurich glittered like an expanse of sequins on a surface of bright blue silk, and at the north end of the lake the red rooftops and slender spires of the town itself basked in the clear joy of a new-born day.

The setting was perfection, but the group of men gathered in the lakeside villa on the edge of the city gave no thought to the magnificence of their surroundings. The wide window behind them directly overlooked the lake and sunlight flooded the room, but their attention was centred inwards.

There were five of them seated around a small conference table. A small business gathering, each with his own blotter and a small glass ashtray, but strangely none of them with a pen or pad, or any means of making notes. Four of them listened while the fifth man talked.

The speaker was a slim, dapper, upright man whose hair was prematurely white. His name was Raab, and even among the shrewd and expert bankers of Zurich he was acknowledged as one of the finest financial brains alive. He owned this lavish villa together with several others, all furnished with the same quiet, tasteful extravagance. He also owned a dozen companies with worldwide interests, and controlling shares in a score of others. He owned a private yacht at Cannes, his own private plane, and alternately drove a Rolls-Royce and a fast Mercedes. He was listed as one of the wealthiest men in the world, and had, or could obtain, literally everything that money could buy.

Now he regarded the four faces turned attentively towards him. Collard, the Belgian; Lemmer, a fellow Swiss; Neumann, the German from Dortmund; and the dark, hook-nosed face that clashed with the Europeans around him, Khalil, whose passport described him as a Libyan businessman. They in their turn had money far beyond their needs, and in the case of Lemmer and Collard they too could have been classed as financial wizards.

But at the moment they were not dealing with the world of high finance, the world they knew so well, and which had initially brought them together. Finance, and the making of still more money, were irrelevant factors with them now. Instead they sat here to form the high council of the organisation that they had christened with the letters A.F.P.

Raab's voice was quiet, and calmly controlled, the voice of a man who had never had to raise his tone to ensure complete attention. He said softly, "That is the position, gentlemen. The British section of our organisation has been smashed. The area controller is dead, and so is the French assassin whom our good friend Khalil recommended. The British security forces moved with astonishing speed after the death of their Prime Minister, although I think that the element of luck must have played a great part in their success."

He stopped there, waiting for comment, and then the guttural Neumann said harshly, "It does not matter. The British section achieved its task. We had no further use for them."

There were nods of agreement, then Lemmer said firmly, "In any case, it is too late to stop now. The main plan must go on."

Raab smiled. "Can I take it that we are all agreed upon that?" His four colleagues each signified assent, and Raab rose to his feet. "In that case," he said, "there is nothing more to discuss. It is far too early for me to offer you a drink, but I shall ring the bell for coffee. In three days we should be able to meet again to toast our absolute and overall success."

CHAPTER 8: A GHOST FROM THE PAST

Simon Larren returned to his flat in Rushlake Terrace and snatched a few hours' sleep before driving the MG down to London Airport. His only luggage was a small suitcase, and having ruined two suits in the past four nights he boarded the plane wearing dark slacks and a light grey sports jacket. It was not an outfit he particularly favoured, and he decided ruefully that if life continued its present pace then his wardrobe would be fully cleaned out in less than a week.

He dozed through the flight south, waking when the stewardess jogged his shoulder after the smooth-flying Vanguard had touched down at Bordeaux. There was a fifteen-minute wait in the transit lounge before the plane took off again, and this time he stayed awake through the next leg to Madrid. Idly he watched the mountains of central Spain as they unrolled slowly beneath the deep carpet of broken cloud, the rugged crests soaring up in an effort to touch the plane. Then the mountains faded behind them, and the airliner descended through the cloud above the great plain that surrounded Madrid, dropping gently towards the airport to the north-east of the city.

There was another delay while the plane was refuelled, and once again the stewardesses efficiently shepherded their flock of passengers over to the transit buildings out of the way. They had forty-five minutes and most of them elected to file into the restaurant for a light meal. Larren absently followed the majority, his mind puzzling, as it had done at regular intervals through the morning, over the possible meaning behind the letters A.F.P.

He didn't notice the woman with the auburn hair as she paused in the doorway directly in front of him. She was fumbling in a smart blue handbag that matched the dark blue costume she was wearing, and his shoulder bumped against her arm, almost causing her to drop it. His hand caught the bag in a fast reflex movement, steadying it before it could slip through her fingers, and he smiled quickly.

"I'm sorry. I was dreaming. I didn't —"

The words suddenly stopped in his throat as he stared into her face. Her eyes were a very light hazel colour beneath fine, slender brows, and her features were fair and slightly refined. The sunlight touched red lights in the auburn hair that flowed smoothly to her shoulders. It was a face from his memory. A face that time had dimmed, yet would never conquer, suddenly springing to vivid life like a ghost from the past.

"What's the matter?"

Her voice was cool, but with a note of concern showing through, a pleasant voice that was neither forward nor reserved. And it broke the spell, for it was definitely not the gay, laughing voice of his beloved Andrea. It could not be, for Andrea had lain buried in a Paris cemetery through all the past bitter years. Larren realised that he was still staring, and that his hand still held rigidly to her handbag, and he forced himself to relax.

"I'm sorry," he said again. "You reminded me of someone."

She laughed nervously. "You're not very original. That's the oldest line in the book." She waited for him to smile, and then her face changed slowly. "That was unkind. It wasn't a line. I *do* remind you of someone."

"Very strongly." He felt awkward and off-balance. "But she died several years ago. I'm sorry that I startled you."

"It doesn't matter." She paused, sensing the hesitation that was still in him, then glanced into the restaurant, where their fellow passengers were rapidly filling the seats. Then she looked back at him and said, "I'm travelling alone, so if you want to share a table with me it's all right." She smiled and added candidly, "I have the feeling that if you don't you'll simply stare at me from a distance all through the meal, and that would be more uncomfortable than having you beside me."

Larren still hesitated, sensing that he was being drained of initiative. Technically he was on assignment, and he knew that Smith would not approve of his risking an involvement with this woman, yet the resemblance to Andrea was too striking for him to turn away.

He returned her smile and said, "Perhaps you're right. I think I probably would stare at you. But I promise that I'll try not to."

He opened the door for her and followed her into the restaurant, staying just behind her as a waiter led them to an empty table. He watched her movements, seeing that she did not quite achieve the supple grace that he remembered from Andrea, and noting that her breasts were perhaps slightly fuller than Andrea's had been. It was only when he faced her that he could take her for Andrea's double.

She glanced up at him as she sat down, knowing that he had been measuring her as she walked, but she said nothing until he had ordered for both of them and the Spanish waiter had moved away. Then she asked quietly, "Were you married to her?"

Larren nodded, glad of the sound of her voice that reminded him he was not looking at his dead wife.

"Do you want to talk about her?"

Larren looked away, turning towards the window where their waiting Vanguard was visible on the runway, a heavy yellow fuel tanker manoeuvring close to its wing. He thought of Andrea, and of the contract camp in the mountains north of Ankara where they had first met. He had been a civil engineer, working with a British company on the construction of a hydro-electric power scheme for the Turkish government, and she had been a journalist searching for a story. It had surprised them both to fall violently and unashamedly in love, and within six months he had made her his bride.

There followed the only period of pure happiness that Larren had ever known. Three years of loving bliss that could only be fully appreciated by a man who had spent most of his past life in loneliness; first the solitary self-dependence of a wartime agent working in hostile, enemy-occupied territory, and then the empty wandering of a man who had returned to find his family and old contacts lost in the London Blitz. Civil engineering had been his pre-war career, and he returned to it, working mostly abroad until he met Andrea a long time later.

Andrea had died violently when a chance meeting with one of Larren's wartime comrades had ended in the man's murder and Andrea had accidentally got in the way. Larren had personally killed the men responsible, tracking them down over the next two years in a search that took him halfway across Europe, and finally to the Far East. His quest had brought him back into contact with British Counter-Espionage, and he had worked for Smith ever since. Now, once again, he relived those three short years that occupied such a hallowed, cherished spot in his memory.

He became aware again of the woman beside him; she still waited patiently for an answer to her last question. He looked into her eyes, and had to tell himself that this was a stranger behind the face he had once known so well. Perhaps later, if there was to be any later, he could tell her about Andrea, but not now. He said quietly, "No. I don't really want to talk about her. Do you mind?"

"Of course not." For a moment she touched his hand, then drew away as their waiter appeared with their order.

The interruption helped Larren to find a sense of balance, and when the man had moved away again he smiled at her more firmly and said, "Considering that we're both English we're being very fast with each other. We haven't even been introduced. My name is Simon Larren."

"And mine —" she hesitated for one fleeting second, and at any other time Larren would have noticed. But he was still moved by the startling likeness to Andrea, and he missed it. She finished quickly, "Mine is Jenny Norwood."

The atmosphere between them became uncertain as they ate the light meal provided, and Larren sensed that Jenny Norwood was beginning to regret the impulse that had invited him to her table. He tried to ease the situation, promoting casual conversation on the flight, the weather and the attractions of Spain, but the slight barrier that had been raised by his first silence remained. She had offered herself as a confidante, and although she had tried hard to hide the fact, she was repulsed by his failure to confide.

However, their embarrassment was short-lived, for it was not long before the air hostesses were marshalling them back into the plane and they separated towards their respective seats. They parted formally, and in a friendly manner, but with just a little relief on both sides. Larren had learned that she too was flying to Tangier, but he did not suggest that they should meet again. Her similarity to Andrea was too disturbing, and he could not afford to distract his mind with ghosts. The past was dead, and it could not be reborn, not even with a woman who wore his dead wife's face.

Less than an hour later the Vanguard crossed high above the Straits of Gibraltar, flying in view of the mighty fortress of The Rock, and then a moment later over the sweeping bay and white town of Tangier. They landed at the airport, and after the inevitable delay for customs and passport control they were admitted into Morocco. Larren disregarded the airport bus, feeling a strange reluctance to brush shoulders once more with Jenny Norwood, and found himself a taxi instead. He went straight to the Taza Hotel in the modern half of the town, and asked for Room 36 as he had been instructed.

Once he was alone in the room he dumped his suitcase and pulled off his necktie with a feeling of relief, for although it was late afternoon the temperature was still up in the hundreds. He glanced into the bathroom and shower, then made a check to ensure that the room was not wired for sound, a routine procedure in any foreign city. When he was satisfied he opened his small suitcase, retrieving his throwing knife from a hidden panel in the side and slipping it inside his jacket. Then he closed the case again as a knock sounded on the door.

He opened it and faced a smiling, dapper man wearing a very pale grey lightweight suit, together with a soft cream shirt and a grey and red spotted bow tie. He carried a short cane and wore a flat straw hat at a jaunty angle. His face was dark, but definitely European, and he favoured a thin, pencil-line moustache.

The stranger regarded him cheerfully and said, "You are Monsieur Larren, *oui*? I am Jacques Chevalier. May I come in?"

Larren shrugged and stood aside. His visitor entered the room, removing his hat and spinning it neatly towards the rack on the wall. He turned as Larren closed the door and twirled his cane expertly in the fingers of his right hand.

"No relation to the famous Maurice," he admitted, smiling. "But the very name Chevalier carries its own reputation, and having been blessed to share it with my illustrious namesake I long ago gave up the struggle of trying not to live up to it."

Larren answered the smile. "Perhaps you should have joined him on the stage. But what can I do for you, Monsieur Chevalier?"

The Frenchman pointed the cane at him. "It is more a matter of what *I* can do for *you*. I am your contact in Tangier."

Larren looked at him blankly.

Chevalier made a gesture of despair. "Ah, you damned English, always so cautious. You were with our friend Smith at half-past five this morning, and to quote his exact words: 'We can manage without you, Larren. I can spare you for the long shot.' *C'est bien*?"

Larren chuckled and held out his hand. *"C'est bien."*

They shook hands warmly, then Chevalier turned and made himself comfortable in the nearest chair. As an afterthought he reached into his jacket pocket and produced an automatic. For a second Larren froze, then Chevalier laughed and threw the gun towards him.

"It is a Smith & Wesson," he explained. "Smith informed me that it is a type to which you are accustomed. I am assuming that you did not take the risk of smuggling your own gun through customs."

"Correct." Larren weighed the gun in his hand, verified that it was loaded, and dropped it into his pocket. "You think of everything."

Chevalier smiled. "This is Tangier. For those who can pay, everything is provided."

"What about a man named Henry Mallory? Can you find him for me?"

"Ah, yes." Chevalier flexed the cane in his hands. "My instructions included a description of this man Mallory, and my — ah — contacts in the city are making enquiries. If your Monsieur Mallory *is* in Tangier, then I can find him." He pointed the cane again. "But you, Monsieur — you do not believe that Mallory is in Tangier. Am I not right?"

"Well, at least you're not wrong. My feeling is that Mallory was probably murdered in England, but it is a possibility that he came here, or at least, to some part of Morocco. As Smith said, I'm playing the long shot."

"And if he is here, and we do find him, what then?"

"We watch him," Larren said simply. "We see who he contacts, or rather who contacts him. Just to pull him in wouldn't do us any good. It's a certainty that he could only tell us about the British section of the organisation we're after, and as we've already smashed that branch it would be pretty pointless."

"I see, and after we have waited for someone to contact him — assuming that we find him first — what do you think will happen then?"

Larren said grimly, "I'm convinced that Henry Mallory is destined to be murdered. He's outlived his usefulness and we know that the organisation he works for is utterly ruthless, and so it's the logical thing for them to do. So, even if he has arrived here and is still alive, I still believe that he will eventually be killed. We won't interfere with that, but we will be around to follow his killers back to their base."

Chevalier closed his eyes and shuddered. "I have a sister," he said, "and once she slept with a Major of the British Army. She told me afterwards that the English are terribly cold, their blood never heats above twelve degrees Centigrade. Now I understand what she meant." He opened his eyes again. "But I suppose it is the right course."

Larren nodded and asked, "If Mallory is in Tangier, how long will it take to find him?"

"How long is a piece of string? It all depends upon how he arrived, and how well he has been hidden." Chevalier leaned forward and smiled. "But that is too pessimistic. I should know by tomorrow, or at least within a few days. My contacts here are widely spread. Of course, if he is not here, but in Casablanca, or Fez or in Marrakech, then it will be much more difficult. I might still find him, but it would take much longer." The dapper Frenchman rose to his feet and continued, "But I will not find him at all by sitting here. I must increase the pressure as you might say. I have friends who even now may be holding the information we seek."

"Can I come along?"

"I would rather you did not. Some of my friends are very wary of strangers; they would be stricken both blind and dumb, especially if their dark minds mistook you for a policeman. You understand, of course?"

Larren nodded. "Of course."

Chevalier smiled. "I sense from your tone that you would rather not be idle. But this time you must be patient and leave matters in my hands. There is nothing you can do until I find your Monsieur Mallory, and so I suggest that you devote your evening to the enjoyment of Tangier. In the medina there are men who will sell you hashish or marijuana, or even their sisters if you ask in the right quarter. Tangier is not quite the fleshpot that it was as an international zone, but the delights are still there for those discerning enough to find them. I regret that I cannot act as your guide, but I feel that I shall have a busy night."

He collected his hat and placed it upon his head at the jaunty angle favoured by his well-known namesake, and smiled cheerfully as he left.

"Don't worry about contacting me," he said from the doorway. "For, as the producer said to the pretty *mademoiselle*, I shall most certainly be contacting you."

CHAPTER 9: A ROOFTOP IN THE MEDINA

It was early morning when the flamboyant Chevalier next appeared. He was dressed as before, except that his cream shirt had been freshly laundered, and his face wore a beaming smile of self-satisfaction. He tipped his hat as he greeted Larren, and again skimmed it neatly on to the rack. He made himself comfortable as Larren closed the door, crossing his legs and reclining in the nearest armchair.

"Well, Monsieur," he asked, "how did you enjoy the sins and vices of wicked Tangier?"

Larren smiled. "I didn't. I merely bought myself a map and made myself familiar with the main streets of the city. Then I came back here just in case you decided to contact me."

"You English," Chevalier said disapprovingly. "Always so conscientious. Even if I had found Mallory last night I could have set a couple of men to watch him. You should have become a tourist while you had the chance. Did not any of the guides offer to take you places?"

"They offered," Larren said. "But I'm a big boy now. I can find my own pleasures when I'm good and ready. I don't need the help of Arab guides."

"Another of your bad English traits; you're too prudish."

Chevalier was too cheerful to be offensive, and Larren merely smiled. "To business," he prompted. "Have you located Henry Mallory?"

"But of course." Chevalier shrugged casually. "Why else would I be here at this ghastly hour? Your Monsieur Mallory has been in Tangier for the past forty-eight hours. He arrived on Tuesday morning on an Air France flight from Paris, and he is now staying at a cheap apartment in the medina."

Larren stared at him, then said slowly, "So Smith was right; they did get him out of England. How did you manage to find him so fast?"

"It was not so very fast," Chevalier said nonchalantly. "I received his description shortly after noon yesterday when I was warned to expect you, and I started my inquiries immediately. That is now seventeen — no, nearly eighteen — hours ago. But as for how I found him — it was not really difficult. I have friends at both the airport and the harbour, observant friends whose fruitful memories can always be helped by a small remuneration. And my friend at the airport recalled an Englishman who could have fitted Mallory's description arriving alone on the Tuesday morning flight. I also have another friend who checked with the driver of the airport bus, and with the taxi drivers who were at the airport that morning. One of the taxi drivers brought this Englishman into the city and dropped him in the Grand Socco, the large square on the edge of the medina. I have yet another friend among the guides in that area — he probably tried to sell you marijuana if you strayed into the Grand Socco last night — and through him I have finally found the place where this Englishman has gone to ground." He smiled and flexed his cane. "It is useful to have friends, is it not? Even though they are friends whom I would not be proud to invite to my home."

"It's definitely an asset," Larren agreed. "But are you sure this Englishman of yours is Henry Mallory?"

Chevalier shrugged his slim shoulders. "The description fits, even down to his moustache. He has not even had the sense to shave it off. And if he were only a tourist he would be staying at one of the hotels, and not hiding in a back alley in the medina." He pointed his cane and added, "The final identification is up to you."

Larren turned the cane aside with his finger. "I wish you wouldn't point that," he said gently. "I get a horrible feeling that a dagger blade might pop out of the end of it."

Chevalier laughed. "You read too many spy novels, my friend. This is just an ordinary cane. But —" he flexed it lovingly — "it can be almost as useful as a blade. A thrust in the right part of the abdomen can cripple a man very effectively, even with the blunt end of a cane."

Larren smiled. "I'll take your word for it. When do I get a look at Mallory?"

"Tout de suite!" Chevalier stood up and snapped his fingers, balancing his cane on his right shoulder. "My car is waiting in the street outside."

Larren took down his jacket from the wall and tossed Chevalier his hat. The Frenchman caught it neatly and carried it in the same sweeping movement to his head.

"All right," Larren said. "Let's go."

They left the hotel and went out into the street, and Chevalier led the way to a large blue-grey Citroen saloon that was parked against the kerb. As they settled themselves inside Chevalier started the engine and said proudly, "I have only had her a month. She is this year's model. She can do one hundred and eighty kilometres per hour, which is about one hundred and twelve of your crazy English miles. She is some car, *oui?* French-made, of course."

"Very nice," Larren said, relaxing against the leather-upholstered seat as the car pulled away. Then he looked across at the Frenchman. "But somewhat ostentatious. Tell me, Jacques, what kind of cover do you have here in Tangier?"

Chevalier smiled, his teeth gleaming below the dark line of his moustache. "I am a nightclub owner. But I will not take you there until this affair is over. I never mix business with business."

He turned the Citroen on to the Avenue D'Espagne, the wide palm-lined road that followed the curving sweep of the bay towards the harbour and the old medina. The sun was high now, and the fierce glare of sea and sky, the golden beach, the bright green of the palms, and the harsh white walls of the town itself, all combined to make Larren squint through narrowed eyes. Veiled women and long-robed men stared at the sleek car as it swished smoothly past, but their eyes were empty of expression. It was just another foreign car in the stream of fast-moving American taxis that hooted their endless, impatient way around the hot, restless streets.

"I have lived in Tangier for twelve years," Chevalier explained. "It was not too difficult to make money in those early years, especially if a man was clever and not too scrupulously honest. And in my modest way I was clever, and my honesty was somewhat doubtful. Then in 1956 Tangier ceased to be an international zone and became part of the independent kingdom of Morocco, and I saw then that the previous opportunities would start to fade. I also foresaw that Tangier would become the tourist attraction that she is today, and so I bought a partnership in my nightclub. My partner was ageing and needed a younger man to shoulder the work, and finally he sold out to me altogether. He now lives quite happily with his mistress in the south of France.

"So, I am now a respectable businessman, but the old, shady contacts still remain, together with the new contacts my position brings from the higher social circles. I am obviously a useful man, and both the French and the British secret services have recognised that. They each pay me a retainer that helps to maintain my circle of contacts, and from time to time, such as this present moment, I dabble in your mysterious world of secret agents."

Larren smiled. He could have commented that Chevalier was no mere dabbler, but he saw no reason to take up the subtle invitation to pander to the man's vanity. Chevalier's ego needed no boosting.

They turned away from the sea front before reaching the harbour, and drove uphill into the Grand Socco. Here Chevalier stopped the Citroen to one side of the square, directly opposite the graceful, rising tower of a mosque. The tower was faced with an elegant pattern of brown and blue mosaic, and the white-walled mosque was roofed with green tiles. The other sides of the square presented an array of tiny, green-shuttered shops set into white walls, and here and there the arched entrances to the jostling alleyways of the medina.

"From here it is easier to walk," Chevalier said, and got out of the car.

Larren joined him, and leaving the Citroen they crossed the square and passed through one of the horseshoe archways into the old Arab town. The street descended steeply, and on either side were a multitude of tiny shops, overflowing with fruit and dates. Then more shops with leather goods and souvenirs, and tiny cafes where dark-robed people sipped at tiny glasses of tea, each glass thick with floating leaves of green mint. They rubbed shoulders with men in harsh brown robes, hooded like medieval monks, and with women hidden like bulky ghosts in white robes that showed only their watching eyes. The chatter and bustle swirled around them as Chevalier led the way deeper into the side streets.

They walked clear of the shops, and into a maze of dull white walls with rough ground or patches of broken cobbles underfoot, and then Chevalier stopped before a solid, bolt-studded door of Moorish design. Larren looked at him questioningly.

Chevalier smiled as he banged the knocker. "Do not worry, my friend. I am not going to confront you directly with Mallory. We have arrived, but he is not in this house."

Larren was intrigued, but he allowed the Frenchman to continue the moment of mystery which he was clearly enjoying. The door opened and a veiled woman peered out cautiously before unhooking a short chain to let them in. The interior was cool but musty, and Chevalier led the way up a bare wooden staircase. A few moments later the sun blinded them again as they came out on to the flat roof.

A young man in a shabby European suit turned sharply to face them, then relaxed as he recognised the Frenchman. He came towards them and Larren saw a pair of binoculars in his hand.

"This is Abdullah," Chevalier said, "one of my more useful friends. He has a very nice sister if you are ever interested, but I don't suppose that you will be."

Abdullah grinned. "I sell heroin too. Pretty cheap."

"A regular delinquent," Chevalier said sadly. "I think he must have been misunderstood in his youth." He reached out to take the binoculars and asked in the same casual tone, "Is the Englishman still there?"

Abdullah nodded vigorously. "He has not left his room. Old Yacoub brought him food up on a tray."

"Très bon!" Chevalier led the way to the waist-high wall that encircled the flat rooftop, and knelt to rest his elbows as he sighted through the binoculars. The surrounding buildings

were of irregular levels, but mostly lower than the one on which they now stood, and so it was possible to see over most of the old town. To their right Larren could see the mosque tower and walls of the old Kasbah, and beyond that a silver-blue glimpse of the sea. To their left and a little behind them was the mosque that marked the Grand Socco, then the larger multi-storeyed blocks of modern Tangier.

Chevalier was still for a moment, and then he handed the binoculars to Larren. "Over there," he said. "About sixty yards away where the window with the white shutters shows through that gap between the two houses."

Larren trained the glasses in the direction of Chevalier's pointing finger, and after a moment focused on the window with the white shutters flung open against the wall. For a few seconds he could see nothing in the shadowy interior of the distant room, but then his vision cleared and he made out the man lying on his back on an old wrought-iron bed. He had to wait another two or three minutes before the man moved his head, and was conscious of the sun pounding down upon the back of his exposed neck. And then at last the man turned his face into focus, and Larren recognised the bluff features and the bushy grey moustache that he had last seen in the London strip club. He lowered the glasses and said flatly, "There's no mistake, Jacques. That's Henry Mallory."

Chevalier smiled his satisfaction, then reached for the glasses and handed them back to the waiting Abdullah. Then he squatted with his back to the wall and said, "And now that we have found him, we wait for him to be killed, *oui*?"

Larren nodded, adopting the Frenchman's example and keeping low. "That's what will happen next," he said. "I'm sure of it. I'm only surprised that he has stayed alive as long as this."

"Perhaps he has reached the same conclusion as you," Chevalier suggested. "Namely that he has served his purpose and is now only an inconvenience, to be disposed of at the first opportunity. He may have deserted his employers as soon as he arrived here, and possibly is now in hiding from them also."

Larren thought about it. "It's possible," he conceded. "But I still have to work on the assumption that someone from this A.F.P. organisation will eventually find him. From now on I'll stay here with Abdullah, or at least —" he squinted skywards and grinned wryly — "I'll stay in the room below. I want to be on hand when anything develops." He paused, then asked, "How long will it take me to reach that building if it becomes necessary?"

"Less than two minutes. There is a practically direct route through an alleyway round the corner of this building. Abdullah can show you."

"Good." Larren smiled. "That means that when Mallory does have visitors I can get there in time to follow them as they leave."

"Possibly." The Frenchman sounded dubious, and Larren looked at him sharply. Chevalier continued, "I think I have a better plan."

"What is it?"

Chevalier smiled and reached into his pocket to produce a heavy gold cigarette lighter. "Simply this, my friend. I have in my possession a miniature homing device, one that is small enough to be concealed inside my cigarette lighter if we first remove some of the wadding. Now, if we do this, and can ensure that Monsieur Mallory finds my cigarette lighter and puts it in his pocket, then the signal from the homer will give us a constant clue to his whereabouts. But, what is even better, if he is to be killed as you expect, then his killers will most certainly search him in order to remove any means of identity, and in doing so they in turn will find my excellent cigarette lighter. It is real gold and very valuable, so they are most certain to keep it, and then it is they who will be carrying the signal that will enable us to trace them. Is this not a better idea?"

Larren said slowly, "It sounds good. But how do we plant the lighter on Mallory in the first place?"

Chevalier shrugged. "It should not be difficult. The room he occupies is above Yacoub's bar, and although he has not left the building since he arrived he does go down to the bar in the evenings and drinks. A drunken Frenchman could leave the lighter on the bar beside him and forget it, and the chances are that Mallory will put it in his pocket. If he is still alive this evening it should be worth a try; even if he proves honest and gives the lighter over to old Yacoub, I can always claim it back later. We shall have lost nothing."

Larren smiled. "You have a tricky mind, but if your scheming works it will certainly make my job much easier. Tonight you can give it a try, and in the meantime I'll remain here."

Chevalier nodded approval. "Abdullah will stay with you. I shall return to my apartment and pick up the little homer bug and the receiver. I'll take a taxi and leave the Citroen parked in the Grand Socco, just in case you need a car in a hurry. Here are the keys."

"Thanks." Larren accepted them as he and Chevalier straightened up. Together they moved away from the encircling wall to the trapdoor in the centre of the roof, and then suddenly Abdullah grabbed at Chevalier's arm.

"Monsieur, the Englishman — he has a visitor."

Chevalier stopped and took the glasses that the young man offered. He did not wait to approach the wall and kneel, but stood upright and trained them across the rooftops. He was still for a moment, then said slowly, "It is a woman. Surely your mysterious organisation would not send a woman to do their killing?"

"All things are possible," Larren said grimly. He accepted the glasses in turn and trained them on the white-shuttered window. At first he could only see Mallory. The man was standing and facing the door, and there was a look of utter astonishment on his face. But there was also recognition and no trace of fear, and it was obvious that whoever his visitor might be she offered him no danger. And then the woman moved into view, and it was Larren's turn to receive a shock of surprise, a shock that stirred a sudden pounding in his heart.

He was staring once again into the face that reminded him so vividly of Andrea. The face of the woman who had introduced herself in Madrid as Jenny Norwood.

CHAPTER 10: STAND ASIDE FOR MURDER

Yacoub's bar was a cheap, spartan place that was littered, rather than furnished, with three bare wooden tables and a handful of rickety chairs. The bar counter was topped with a slab of heavy marble that was chipped and cracked around the edges, behind which presided Yacoub himself in a drab grey djellaba and a red fez. The walls were relieved by an old calendar, a faded Coca-Cola sign and a framed photograph of King Hassan of Morocco. Most of the customers were locals, sitting at the tables and gossiping as they sipped their mint tea. Behind the bar Yacoub also stocked soft drinks for those who wanted something iced, and a small supply of bottled beers for the occasional non-believers who were not Muslims.

At the far end of the bar Henry Mallory stood alone, an outcast, and not one of the faithful, the fact marked by the beer on the counter before him. He badly needed something stronger, but Yacoub kept no spirits and he was afraid to go outside and seek out another bar. He was afraid even standing here, but he had always been prey to claustrophobia and he needed the brief respite from the cramped prison of his room. In the past three days his bluff, hearty face had lost most of its colour, and now he looked exactly what he was: a sick and badly worried man.

His whole body flinched as the curtain was pushed back in the doorway behind him, the brass rings scratching loudly along the supporting rail. He turned and saw a dapper little man in a pale grey suit and a flat straw hat entering the bar.

The man swayed forward, obviously drunk, and rapped playfully on the counter with a short cane.

"Cognac," he demanded. "And afterwards you can tell me how to find my way out of this maze of streets and back to the harbour."

Yacoub shuffled forward. "Only beer," he said slowly. "Beer or tea."

Chevalier blinked owlishly. "But I want cognac."

The old man frowned, his forehead creasing below the sharp line of his fez. "There is only beer," he repeated.

Chevalier stared at him, seemingly unaware of the dark faces of the customers casting disapproving glances in his direction. Then he beamed, and spread his hands in an expansive gesture. "All right — pour me a beer."

Yacoub nodded, and served him with deliberate slowness. Chevalier paid him and then twisted his face distastefully as he tasted the drink. He looked round the bar and noticed Mallory.

"Bonjour!" he cried cheerfully. "I spy another tourist." He shifted along the bar, stumbling slightly, and finished up by Mallory's side. "What do you think of this place, eh? Tangier, the city of sin and wickedness — and you cannot even buy a glass of cognac." He tasted his beer again and grimaced ruefully. Then he looked at Mallory. "You know, I shall be glad to get on board the ship again; at least they have a decent bar aboard. And I thought that Tangier was to be the best port of the cruise. Pah!" He lowered his glass and fumbled in his pocket for a cigarette case. "After that I need something to take the taste away," he proclaimed. "Will you join me?"

Mallory hesitated. He had hoped that his silence would drive his unwanted companion away, but he could not risk an outright quarrel by being rude. He forced a weak smile and accepted a cigarette from the offered case.

"Thank you."

Chevalier beamed at him and selected a cigarette for himself before slipping the case away. Then he took out his heavy gold lighter and lit them both. He put the lighter on the counter and picked up his glass again.

"Casablanca was better," he said. "Much better than Tangier. And Tenerife and Las Palmas, they were good places. But now we return to Marseilles —" He talked on volubly, spilling out details of a fictional pleasure cruise while Mallory fidgeted awkwardly and made polite comments.

For another ten minutes Chevalier chattered on, and then he drained the last of his beer and glanced at his wristwatch. *"Oh, mais non!"* he exclaimed frantically. "Look at the time. I must be back aboard the ship before thirty minutes." He grabbed Mallory by the arms. "Quickly, you must tell me, how do I find my way back to the harbour? I am lost in these damned back alleys."

Mallory looked confused, and inside he was frightened of the attention they were attracting. He said uncertainly, "Bear left, I think. If you keep going that way you should get back to the big square. You can find a taxi there. That's your best plan."

"*Ah, merci, Monsieur.* And now I must run." Chevalier patted him gratefully on the shoulder and turned unsteadily to make for the door. He waved an owlish goodbye as he went through the curtains, and then he was lost from sight.

Henry Mallory breathed a sigh of deepest relief, and decided that it was time that he too escaped to the safety of his room. He turned to go, and then he saw the expensive gold cigarette lighter still sitting on the bar counter.

For a moment he hesitated, then he picked it up and hurried to the door. He passed through the curtains and stopped in the empty street outside. Already the drunken Frenchman had vanished.

Again Mallory was uncertain and confused. Basically he was an honest man, and in ordinary circumstances he would have undoubtedly handed the gold cigarette lighter to the nearest policeman, but now he had good reasons for avoiding the police. He thought for a moment of handing it to Yacoub, but if the Frenchman was rushing to catch a boat then obviously he was unlikely to ever return, so there was no point in making a present of his property to the old man. Mallory finally thought of his own position, and of the fact that his money was slowly running out. He crushed down his principles then and accepted the gift from fate, dropping it into his pocket as he turned back into the bar and climbed the stairs to his room above.

Sixty yards away, across the rooftops, Simon Larren leaned against the encircling wall and stared upwards at the night sky. Below him the narrow, darkened streets of the medina were silent and mostly empty, but in the heavens a million stars glittered with vast, hypnotic beauty. Abdullah had left him for a while, and now he was alone with his thoughts.

There was no light in the room occupied by Mallory, and so the binoculars that still dangled from Larren's hand were now useless to him. He could only trust that Chevalier was keeping watch on the man he wanted, but he had faith in the egoistic little Frenchman and he was not worried. He had allowed himself to relax, savouring the coolness of the night after the day's fierce heat.

His thoughts were still haunted by the face that had appeared once again as a reincarnation of his beloved Andrea, and he was still disturbed by emotions he had long believed dead.

Several times throughout the day he had watched her through binoculars, seeing her argue and remonstrate with Mallory, although it was impossible to guess at what was being said. They had both appeared pale and worried, and once her anguished face had been streaked with tears. Mallory had kissed her then, gently upon the forehead as he held her close, and Simon Larren had felt a sharp stab of what could only have been jealousy as he watched.

Her presence was a mystery, and although causing Mallory some agitation she was now sharing his room. Larren knew that she was almost certainly in there now, even though Mallory would be in the bar below, and the thought refused to leave his mind. She had awakened a lost love, and its memories stirred a longing from the past. He had known many women since Andrea had died, but none of them had been of any importance. They had been simply bodies to be enjoyed. Now he felt that his capacity for real love might still be revived, except that now it was too late and could not be allowed. The years with Counter-Espionage had left too much blood on his hands.

He brooded in silence, and was almost glad when the sound of movement from below the open trapdoor in the centre of the roof finally claimed his attention. He watched as the familiar outline of the flat straw hat came into view, and then Chevalier climbed out on to the roof to join him. The Frenchman was smiling broadly.

"Monsieur Mallory has taken the bait," he said softly. "He followed me out of the bar with my gold lighter in his hand, but when he found that he could not catch me he gave way to temptation and eventually put it in his pocket. I was watching from the shadows of the next alleyway."

He produced what at first looked like a pocket-sized transistor radio, and deftly pressed a switch. Immediately a soft bleeping signal ensued, and a thin needle on a small dial trembled before swinging to point in the direction of Yacoub's bar.

"Excellent," Chevalier murmured. "He is now back in his room and the transmitter is working perfectly. Wherever Mallory goes now we can follow him, and stay well out of sight."

"Provided that he keeps the transmitter in his pocket," Larren reminded him.

"But of course. We will not rely wholly upon my little homer bug. We will continue to watch from here by day, and by night I have a man watching the bar from an alleyway; one of Abdullah's many cousins. The homer bug is merely an additional precaution." Chevalier smiled fondly at his small receiver, and then he turned down the sound to a minimum to avoid attracting any attention.

"There is more news," he added casually as the bleeping died away. "London has finally answered your request for information on this girl who calls herself Jenny Norwood. One of my waiters from the nightclub was waiting below with the message when I returned just now from Yacoub's bar. It seems that there really is a Jenny Norwood, and that she is a niece of Henry Mallory's. However, our friend Smith has prompted some investigations, and has discovered that the genuine Jenny Norwood is still living at her home in Croydon. She has been questioned and has now admitted that the woman travelling with her passport is in fact her cousin, Henry Mallory's daughter, Barbara." Chevalier paused, then concluded, "Barbara Mallory must have realised that she and her mother would be watched by your Special Branch in case her father tried to contact them, and so she used her cousin's passport to join him. Apparently the two girls are approximately the same age and very similar in appearance. It is a pity, for if her father is to be killed, then poor Mademoiselle Mallory may share his fate."

Larren inclined his head slowly, his face unsmiling and expressionless, but inside a cold web had formed around his heart.

The night passed uneventfully. There was no change in either the direction finder or the homing signal from the receiver, and no word from Abdullah's cousin who watched Yacoub's bar. Larren spent the night on the rooftop where it was cooler and fresher than the rooms below, dozing lightly but never fully asleep. At dawn he was wide awake and went back to the routine of studying Mallory's window every few minutes through the binoculars. An hour later Abdullah appeared, looking fresh for duty and explaining that his cousin had now packed up the night shift and gone home.

Larren remained on the roof, feeling reluctant to hand over the binoculars to the young man. Through the open window across the rooftops he could now see Barbara Mallory lying asleep on the old-fashioned bed, while her father slept restlessly on the floor of the room beyond. They were both fully dressed, but even so Larren felt very much a Peeping Tom as he spied upon them, and he could not bring himself to pass the glasses to a man who sold his sister. Abdullah seemed unconcerned, and simply squatted in the shade of a low wall and smoked a cheap cigarette.

At last Barbara Mallory stirred and sat up. A spasm of worry passed across her face for a moment as she looked down at her sleeping father, and then she stood up and crossed quietly to a small washbasin that stood upon a low table on the far side of the room. Larren lowered the binoculars as she started to remove her blouse, and gave her five minutes to complete her toilet before he raised them again. By then she was dressed once more and shaking Mallory by the shoulder to wake him up. Larren passed Abdullah the glasses and relaxed.

Soon after that Chevalier returned, bringing with him some English newspapers, a large packet of ham sandwiches and a flask of coffee. They conferred for a moment, then the Frenchman apologised for the fact that he had to depart almost immediately. There were some minor staff problems with his nightclub that needed smoothing over, but he promised to return within an hour to share in the task of keeping watch.

After Chevalier had left Larren used the binoculars again to look into Mallory's room. He saw that Barbara Mallory was preparing to leave, and seemed to be trying to reassure her father upon some point. He wished that he could lip-read, and watched until she kissed Mallory on the cheek and then turned away. Mallory watched the door close behind her, then sat down wearily on the bed. His face looked grey and old, and his heavy body seemed to have visibly shrunk.

Larren wondered for a moment whether to send Abdullah to follow the woman, but then he decided against it. Only Mallory himself was important. He watched the man for a few minutes longer, but Mallory had settled down and showed no signs of moving.

The harsh North African sun was now beating down with its full morning violence, and there was no longer any shade upon the rooftop. The blue sky and the white walls of the buildings reflected its glare from every angle into Larren's aching eyes and he knew that it was time he gave himself a break. Abdullah seemed careless of the heat, and Larren envied him as he gave the youth the glasses and went below.

He drank the coffee that Chevalier had brought him, and ate most of the sandwiches. He was confident that Abdullah would warn him if anything happened, and afterwards he relaxed and turned his attention to the newspapers. They were dated the previous day, and were mostly full of the preparations for the Prime Minister's state funeral, and it was with something of a shock that Larren realised that almost a week had passed since Sir Howard Davies had been assassinated. Today was again Friday, and the funeral was scheduled to take place on the following afternoon.

There were large photographs of the draped coffin lying in state, and long, impressive lists of the crowned heads of Europe, Commonwealth leaders and heads of state gathered from all over the world to attend its last procession. The President of the United States was due to fly into London on a late-night flight from New York, and Zuchev, the present top man of the Supreme Soviet, would be arriving from Moscow shortly after dawn. It was a noted tribute that the leaders of both East and West were to attend personally instead of merely sending a representative.

Larren turned the pages of both papers and then pushed them aside, contemplating for a moment on the amount of upheaval that could be caused by one single bullet. And not least among the consequences was his own presence here in Tangier. The full circle of his thoughts brought him back to the job in hand, and he decided that it was time he relieved Abdullah.

He started up the ladder to the roof, wincing as the sun's glare struck at his eyes. Then, abruptly, the shadow of Abdullah fell over him.

"Come quickly," the youth hissed. "Something is happening."

Larren scrambled up the ladder fast, grabbing the binoculars as Abdullah led him back to the wall. He knelt and clamped them to his eyes, but it was a moment before his vision adjusted and he was able to see. Then he picked up Mallory's window again and held the glasses steady.

Two men had entered Mallory's room, two dark-faced men in lightweight European suits. One stood just inside the door, his features blank but watchful, while the other had approached the Englishman and was speaking softly. Mallory's face was hidden, for his back was towards the window, but there was the stiffness of terror in his rigid body, and Larren knew that the moment they had all awaited had come at last.

He focused the binoculars on each of the distant faces in turn, committing them indelibly to his memory, and then he turned and faced Abdullah.

"Stay here and keep watch," he ordered. "And when Chevalier returns tell him everything that has happened. I'm going over to the bar ready to follow those two men when they come out."

Abdullah nodded energetically. "I can do."

Larren smiled and gave him the glasses, then hurried across the roof and swung himself down the ladder. It took him a matter of seconds to reach the street, and immediately he broke into a run, zigzagging between startled men and their white-robed women. A donkey loaded down with two heavy straw panniers cost him valuable seconds where it jammed the narrow alleyway, but even so he reached the front of Yacoub's bar in under two minutes. He pressed back into an alley mouth, panting slightly, and waited.

He did not have to wait long. Another minute ticked by, and then there was a movement in the doorway of the bar. The man who had stood with his back to Mallory's door stepped out into the sunlight and stood with his hand shielding his eyes until his companion joined him. The second man coolly tightened the knot of his silk tie as he straightened his shoulders, then both of them strolled calmly away.

They turned a corner, heading towards the Grand Socco, and the moment they were out of sight Larren moved across the street and ducked into the bar. The gloomy interior was like a dark cave, but he spotted the staircase at the far end of the room and ran towards it. Old Yacoub watched as he dashed upwards, standing among the tables with a broom in his hand. Then he shook his head in sad bewilderment and went back to his sweeping.

Larren reached the top of the staircase, and paused outside the door of Mallory's room. The door was slightly ajar, and he pushed it slowly open. His hand was in his jacket pocket, gripping the Smith & Wesson that Chevalier had so thoughtfully provided, but the gun was not needed. Henry Mallory was alone in the room, and Mallory was very definitely dead.

Larren moved into the room and crouched by the body on the floor. The ex-Member of Parliament lay on his back close to the ancient iron bed; his heavy body was slack and crumpled and fear was frozen with agony into his last expression. The black powder burns around the bullet wound in his left breast showed that he had been shot at close range, and Larren guessed that it had been done with a silenced gun.

He went swiftly through the dead man's pockets, knowing that he had time to catch up with the killers before they reached the Grand Socco. He found nothing that could identify the man, but a smile of satisfaction touched his lips when he found that Chevalier's gold cigarette lighter was also missing.

He was ready to leave them, but as he withdrew his hand from the inside pocket of Mallory's jacket he heard a movement in the doorway behind him. There was a startled gasp of indrawing breath, and Larren's hand dived instinctively for the Smith & Wesson. He twisted in the same moment, still balancing on one knee, and found himself face to face with Barbara Mallory.

She stood just inside the door with her shoulders backed against the wall.

Her hazel-coloured eyes were wide with horror and her mouth was trembling violently, yet somehow the blunt-nosed automatic in her hand was staying steady as it pointed between his eyes.

CHAPTER 11: DEAD MAN'S DAUGHTER

Larren stayed perfectly still, knowing that he was as close to death at this moment as he had ever been in the whole of his violent and bloody career. He crouched beside the body of Henry Mallory, and even his breathing stopped as he stared up at the dead man's daughter. The Smith & Wesson was still in his right hand, but he knew that if he levelled it to fire then he would die instantly. Barbara Mallory was frozen almost as rigid as he was, and only her face twisted and shook, quivering with unshed tears. She was wearing the dark blue costume in which he had first seen her, and her knuckles were white around the gun.

For over a minute neither of them moved, the woman rooted by shock, and Larren fearful of breaking the slender thread of silence upon which his life depended. Then Larren drew a slow breath, and with the microscopic care of a surgeon he slowly moved the Smith & Wesson. He lowered it until it was pointing to the floor, then opened his fingers and gently let it drop. The sound made her flinch, but apart from that she still didn't move.

Larren said quietly, "I didn't kill him, if that's what you're thinking. He was dead when I arrived."

"You murdered him!" The words were a sharp explosion between her lips, and once the dam had burst they rushed blindly on. "I remember you. You were on the plane from London. You told me some stupid sob story at Madrid, and like a silly little fool I believed you. And all the while it was you he was afraid of. It was you he was running away from. And you followed me — you used me to find him. You killed him. You murderer!" She took a step forward and it was Larren's turn to flinch, but then she regained some element of control and tears flooded her eyes as she demanded bitterly, "Why did you kill him? Why?"

"I didn't kill him," Larren said flatly, and suddenly it was important that he convinced her. Not because his own life now hung in the balance, but because he could not bear the loathing accusation in her eyes. He went on desperately, "It's true that I was following him. I was sent out from London to find him. But I had no idea of who you were when I spoke to you at Madrid. I didn't use you — and I didn't kill him." He saw that at least she was listening, but her expression told him that mere denials were not enough and that he had to make some attempt to explain his own presence here.

He continued bluntly: "Your father was a member of an extremist organisation that calls itself the A.F.P. It was that organisation that planned the assassination of Sir Howard Davies, and your father had some small part in the P.M.'s death. That was why he had to leave England, and that was why I was sent after him. But his own people got to him first. They killed him."

"I don't believe you." Her voice was harsh, almost a sob. "I know he was running away from something, and I know that he was afraid for his life. That's why he made me have this gun, because when I came here he was afraid for me too. But it's a foul lie to say he had anything to do with the death of the Prime Minister. Whatever he did, it couldn't have been as bad as that — it couldn't possibly have been."

"But it was." Larren was beginning to sweat. "Perhaps he didn't realise what they intended to do, but it was your father who notified them that Sir Howard was almost certain to be at the Tempest Club that night." He knew better than to believe the implication that Mallory might have been innocent, but this was no time for pure truth and blatantly he told another lie. "When he realised the truth he must have turned against them. That was why he was running. That was why he was killed."

For a moment it looked as though she might be wavering, and Larren tried a fresh track. He said slowly, "Don't be afraid now. I'm going to reach for my gun and push it across the floor towards you. If you pick it up and smell the barrel you'll find that it hasn't been fired."

"No!"

Her arm thrust forward as she uttered the cry, and Larren froze again as he looked into the death's eye of her automatic. She said hysterically, "If you reach for that gun you'll try and shoot me. You're nothing but a filthy murderer, and you're not fit to live. You've just killed the most wonderful man in the world, and now I'm going to kill you."

In another moment she would have pulled the trigger, and Larren honestly thought that he saw the shadow of death by her shoulder. But the shadow moved, and it was not the gleaming scythe of the grim reaper that cut through the air, but the sharp swish of a slender cane. The automatic was struck smartly from Barbara Mallory's hand, and as it spun to the floor a stronger hand cut off her yelp of pain and she was seized from behind.

Chevalier held her firmly and remarked, "It is fortunate that I hurried back as I promised. It does not seem that you can manage without me."

Larren exhaled slowly, and was ashamed of the weakness in his knees as he straightened up from his cramped crouching position. "Thanks, Jacques," he said warmly. "Remind me to buy you a drink if we ever get the time."

"It will be a large cognac," Chevalier warned him. Barbara struggled in his arms, and he tightened his grip as he added, "But Mademoiselle Mallory is a complication. What shall we do with her?"

Larren hesitated. "We've lost enough time, perhaps too much. We'll have to take her with us."

Chevalier frowned. "It would be better to knock her on the head."

Larren faltered again, then snapped, "No. She'll only have the police baying on our heels the moment she wakes up, and that will be an even bigger complication. Besides —" he felt that his decision needed still more justification — "she might be able to help us. We can talk to her in the car."

Chevalier regarded him dubiously, and Larren suddenly wondered whether he would have been more agreeable to rougher tactics if Barbara Mallory had not reminded him so strongly of Andrea. Then the Frenchman nodded.

"All right, you take her. I'll tell Yacoub that Monsieur Mallory is feeling ill and is not to be disturbed until we return. With luck that will keep him away from this room for a few hours."

Larren felt a sense of relief and smiled his approval, then he quickly collected up the two fallen guns and relieved Chevalier of the now badly frightened woman. She winced as he gripped her arm, but she made no attempt to cry out as the Frenchman tentatively removed his hand from her mouth.

Larren said firmly, "You're not going to be hurt, but you can help us catch the men who killed your father. Please try and believe that."

She said nothing, but the resistance had drained out of her and she allowed him to propel her out of the room.

Chevalier locked the door behind them and pocketed the key, then all three hurried down the stairs. Larren quickly hustled the woman across the bar and out into the street, giving her no chance to recover from her present state of mental confusion. Chevalier hung back and talked earnestly with the old man who had looked up from pottering behind his bar.

A few moments later Chevalier caught up with them as Larren steered the woman at a fast pace through the baffling maze of streets. The Frenchman immediately took the lead and followed the most direct route out of the medina. They reached the busy area around the Grand Socco, and practically ran into the square itself. The blue-grey Citroen was still waiting where they had left it, and Chevalier slid swiftly behind the wheel while Larren bundled the woman into the back.

Barbara pulled away from Larren the moment that he released her arm, flinching away into the far corner of the car. But she did not attempt to escape through the far door and simply stared with grief-dulled eyes as he pulled the homing receiver from his pocket. He switched it on and smiled as the bleeping signal sounded steadily and clearly. He waited for the dial pointer to settle in one direction and then said, "Approximately south-east, Jacques. They must be heading out of Tangier on the Rue de Fez."

Chevalier started the engine and the Citroen pulled smoothly forward. He put his foot down and asked, "How long a start have they got?"

"No more than five minutes. I would have been right behind them if Miss Mallory had not interrupted me."

Chevalier drove fast, handling the big Citroen with a skill born of long experience in the town he knew so well. He took advantage of every gap in the traffic stream, and narrowly avoided a head-on crash with a donkey cart that ambled unexpectedly from a side street. Then they were roaring down the wide, practically straight Rue de Fez.

"What bearing now?" he queried, carelessly throwing a scare into a wobbling cyclist balancing a block of ice upon his handlebars. "Is it south, or still moving south-east?"

Larren said quietly, "Still south-east."

"Then it is not Rabat," Chevalier observed. "They must be making for Tetouan. I had the feeling that our killers would come from outside Tangier. If it had not been so they would have found him much sooner."

Larren remained silent, making no comment to distract Chevalier from his handling of the car. They turned left on to the Boulevard Moulay Youssef, then swung right again as they entered the wide Place d'Europe. Then they were leaving the town behind them and heading for open country on the main road to Tetouan. The homer signal was bleeping strongly, and the direction pointer was reading directly ahead.

Larren relaxed now that they were on the open road, and glanced briefly at the woman. She had recovered some of her composure, and although her feelings were still stunned by shock she was losing a little of her fear. He saw that within a few moments she would be asking questions, and forestalled them by speaking first.

"Did your father ever tell you anything about the men who were hunting for him?" he asked her quietly.

She looked at him, and for a moment he thought that she would turn away and refuse to answer, but then she breathed deeply and said, "He wouldn't tell me very much. I tried to help him but he didn't want me to know. He just said that he was in some kind of trouble in England, but I knew that because we had some detectives come to the house looking for him. His picture was in the papers too, but they just said that the police wanted to find him because he had gone missing." She swallowed hard and then finished, "If — if it was something to do with the Prime Minister being killed, then — then it was all a mistake. Someone must have tricked him into helping them."

Larren did not respond to that, for there was nothing to be gained in destroying the last of the dead man's image. Instead he posed another question: "Did he tell you how he managed to get out of England and make his way here to Tangier?"

She nodded. "He said that some friends helped him to get across the Channel in a small boat. They gave him another passport in a different name, and after that he took a plane from Paris. But when he arrived in Tangier he felt that he couldn't even trust his friends any more. He was frightened, so instead of going to the hotel address they had given him he found that dirty little room in the medina. He was hiding there. He didn't know what to do next."

She turned her face away suddenly, and although she was silent Larren knew that there were fresh tears staining her cheeks. He was stirred by compassion, and with it there was even a grain of pity for the trapped and desperate fugitive that had been her father. Henry Mallory's web had been of his own making, but it had left him friendless and ensnared him cruelly.

Larren gave her time to recover herself, then asked, "How did you know where to find him?"

"He sent us a letter." The answer came slowly but without hesitation. "Not directly of course, because he was afraid that it might have been intercepted by the police. He sent it to my cousin, and she passed it on to me. He only wanted to tell us that he was all right, and that we were not to worry about him. He didn't say where he was, but the letter had a Moroccan stamp and a Tangier postmark, so it didn't take much working out."

"And the cousin who received the letter was the real Jenny Norwood," Larren presumed. "And so you borrowed her passport and came to find your father."

She nodded. "It wasn't very hard. A few years back he made a short tour of Gibraltar with some other M.P.s, and afterwards he took a couple of days' holiday and made a quick visit to Tangier. He found Yacoub's bar then, when he got lost in the medina, and I've heard him mention it. I guessed that if he was afraid to use a hotel then he'd make for the only place he knew, and so I asked one of the guides in the Grand Socco to take me there."

Larren glimpsed something of her inner courage and felt a new respect for the woman beside him. "What did you hope to do?"

"To help him somehow. I don't know how. When I found that he was afraid of someone coming after him here I thought that he should move. I went to the railway station this morning to find out what times the trains left for Rabat and Casablanca. It wasn't a final answer, but it seemed a start. I thought he might loosen up and explain more if we could get to somewhere where he would feel safe."

She became silent again, and Larren felt that he had worried her with enough questions. He left her to grieve, and then Chevalier spoke abruptly from the driving seat. "There is a car ahead. I think this is it."

Larren stared over the Frenchman's shoulder at a wide, American convertible stirring up the dust ahead of them. It was still a long way in front, but he could make out the outlines of two passengers and a driver. He checked the homing signal and realised that the bleeping was now at full strength. He turned it down and said, "That's the one all right."

Chevalier nodded, and slowed the Citroen to stay well behind. Larren continued to watch over his shoulder, but became suddenly conscious of the fact that Barbara Mallory was staring at the receiver in his hand. "What is that thing?" she demanded. "How is it following those men in front?"

"It's called a homer," Larren explained. "It's picking up a signal from a miniature transmitter that we concealed in a gold cigarette lighter. They helped themselves to the lighter after they'd killed your father and searched his body."

Her eyes moved to Chevalier. "Then he was the man who left that cigarette lighter in the bar last night. It was left there deliberately."

Larren saw the horror dawning in her eyes, but by then it was too late to rectify the blunder he had made. He cursed himself inwardly and was incapable of saying anything.

"You didn't just find my father; you've been watching him." Her voice shuddered and almost broke. "You've been watching him and waiting for this to happen. You even planted that homer thing on him so you could follow his killers. You wanted him to be killed. You could have stopped it, but you just stood by and let it happen." She screamed suddenly, "Oh, God, you're not even human!"

Larren struck her, hating himself for it, but knowing that within another moment she would have been hysterical. Her cheek flushed bright scarlet under the stinging blow and she fell back against the car's upholstery. Her eyes still stared through the rush of tears, and he knew that only lies would control her.

"We didn't want him killed," he said fiercely, hating himself again for his own deceit. "We simply wanted to watch him and follow him when he went out. We thought he would lead us to his friends, but we didn't expect them to kill him. It was just chance that they took over the transmitter we planted."

She said nothing, but continued to stare at him. He wanted to turn away, anything but face her, but that would have been fatal and he held her gaze. Then slowly the panic faded from her petrified eyes, and he knew that she believed him. It made her calmer, but it also filled his own stomach with a wave of self-revulsion.

Then Chevalier said sharply, "The car is stopping. They are turning off the road."

Larren turned his attention to the road ahead and saw that the open-topped convertible was indeed slowing and turning to the left. There was no track or road, and the big car bumped and rocked as it rolled over open country. It climbed the slope of a hill, balanced for a moment on the skyline, and then dipped out of sight.

Chevalier had automatically slowed the Citroen, and he continued to approach the spot where the other car had left the road at a slow crawl. He stopped where the indentations of the first car's tyres cut deeply into the grass verge, then switched off the engine.

"I think," he said slowly, "that we had better leave the car here until we find out what is happening. We will make ourselves too obvious if we drive straight over that rise in pursuit."

Larren nodded, and together they got out of the car. He quietly warned Barbara to stay where she was as Chevalier came round the nose of the Citroen to join him, then they followed the tyre tracks across the rough ground. Chevalier had pocketed the keys so that Barbara could not drive off without them, and as there was nowhere for her to run to, Larren was confident that she would wait in the back seat.

It was now almost noon, and the blazing sun made them both sweat as they toiled up the slope. They went more warily as they neared the top, and finally wormed the last few yards on their stomachs. They lay side by side as they peered over the hill, and Larren felt a spasm of futile anger as he stared down the far side.

The terrain below them sloped down into a great natural bowl, and at the bottom of the bowl stood the American convertible. But, what was worse, beside it stood a smart four-seater aeroplane. The sun glinted on the sharp lines of the red-and-white-painted fuselage, and made brilliant mirrors of the pure white wings. She was one of the Piper range of light aircraft, and although Larren could not be positive he would have said a Piper Cherokee.

Four men stood between the car and the plane, holding a hurried conversation. One was obviously the pilot and the other three were the men from the convertible. It was obvious that the plane would at any moment whisk the two killers out of reach, while the car driver would run his vehicle back to Tangier, and Larren cursed savagely.

Chevalier glanced at him, then said softly, "All is not yet lost, my friend. I know of another plane within half an hour of here that might be available. If we move fast it is just possible that we can get in the air before they get out of signal range."

Larren stared at him. "Do you mean that?"

"But of course. There is a young Englishman who owns an old Fairchild Argus. He makes his living flying pleasure flights over the bay. We have an understanding, and he has helped me before. Usually the Argus is kept fuelled, and if he is not flying then I am certain that for me he will oblige."

Larren hesitated, and Chevalier continued: "It is your choice. We can charge down there in the Citroen and try to stop them, but we should probably fail. And in any case, what we really want is to track them back to their base. On the other hand, we do risk losing them altogether if they get beyond the range of our receiver before we ourselves can get airborne. It is a gamble."

The alternatives flickered through Larren's mind. It was unlikely that they could stop the Cherokee from taking off before they reached it, and although they probably would be able to grab the car driver who would be left behind, he doubted whether that individual would be of any help. Almost certainly the car driver had only been hired for the one job. He made his decision and wriggled backwards down the slope.

"Let's gamble," he said. "And I hope your friend doesn't let us down."

"My friends never let me down," Chevalier retorted almost indignantly.

They retreated from the hilltop and raced swiftly back to the waiting Citroen.

CHAPTER 12: DESERT FLIGHT

"What's the name of this pilot?"

Larren asked the question as Chevalier hurled the Citroen back along the dusty road to Tangier, driving even more frenziedly than before. The flat vaudeville hat was tilted forward to shadow the Frenchman's narrowed eyes, and he answered absently as he concentrated his mind on the car.

"His name is Gerry Powell. He's an ex-R.A.F. type. He served eight years before his father died and left him with enough money to buy himself out and set himself up with the Argus. One of his tours of duty was at Gibraltar; he was stationed there for three years. That was when he first explored Tangier. He liked the town, the climate, and the people, and so he decided to come back. He's only been out here a few months so it's pretty much a shoestring business. Anyway, he's happy — and I suppose that that is what counts."

"How did you meet him?"

Chevalier shrugged. "The usual way. He came into my club one night, and as he was obviously a useful man to know, I made it my business to get to know him. He hires the plane out occasionally, and I have been able to steer customers in his direction. In return he has helped me." He risked a brief smile over his shoulder. "It is a case of you scratch my fleas and I'll scratch yours."

Larren smiled, but said no more as Chevalier returned his attention to his driving, for once again they were entering Tangier. Chevalier veered to the right, skirting the outskirts of the town and then accelerating again as they raced around the curve of the magnificent bay. Tangier lay behind them as they headed out towards Cap Malabata, where the lonely sentinel of a lighthouse marked the point where the land ended in the sea.

Halfway round the curve of the bay Chevalier stamped hard on the brake pedal, causing the tyres to screech in protest as he pulled the Citroen to a stop. He turned on to a narrow, bare dirt track that led directly away from the sea, and the car swayed and jolted wildly as he revved the engine once again. Larren was thrown against Barbara Mallory, but apart from the slight gasp as he pressed against her she said nothing. She had remained silent and uncommunicative ever since he and Chevalier had scrambled back into the car. He had told her what was happening, but she had made no comment.

After almost a mile of the rough track Larren saw the airfield ahead. It was no more than a flat field, the emptiness broken by two one-storey wooden buildings, a windsock on its pole, and the plane itself, standing stationary in the centre of the field. A large, brightly painted board greeted them as they drew up with the words POWELL'S PLEASURE FLIGHTS.

Below was a list of prices for hour and half-hour flights, but Larren did not bother to read them. He was staring with a sinking heart at the old Fairchild Argus. She looked squat and clumsy compared to the sleek lines of the Cherokee, the fuselage was more tubby and her nose was blunt. Even if they got her in the air in time, she did not look capable of keeping up with the trim little plane carrying Henry Mallory's killers.

Chevalier, however, seemed to have no disillusions. He stopped the Citroen with a jerk outside the first of the two wooden buildings, which now proved to be the booking office, and already he was out of the car. A surprised youth, looking vaguely similar to Abdullah, had watched them arrive from the narrow veranda, and now a tall ginger-headed man came out to join him.

The tall man wore faded blue jeans and a white tee-shirt, and despite sun-browned arms and face he carried the definite stamp of an Englishman. His tousled ginger hair had a wild, schoolboyish look and his eyes were a crisp blue. He looked to be about thirty, and had the easy smile of a man who was satisfied with life, at least for the time being.

"Jacques," he grinned amiably. "What ill wind blows you out here to disturb my peace? Don't tell me that you've actually found me some customers!"

"Not exactly." Chevalier reached the veranda and laid a hand impulsively on the pilot's arm. "Gerry, this is important. How long will it take you to get your plane airborne?"

Powell shrugged. "A matter of minutes. She's all fuelled up. All I need is business."

"Then take us up. We will explain in the air."

"Sure — but why the big rush?"

"Gerry, every second is vital. Quickly now. Trust me."

Powell hesitated, but the urgency of Chevalier's tone had registered, and he made up his mind fast. "Hamid," he snapped at the youth, "I'm going flying. You take care of things till I get back."

The boy nodded and Powell reached into the office for his jacket and a peaked cap. He jammed the cap on his head and allowed Chevalier to hustle him away from the veranda.

Larren was waiting for them and still gripping Barbara's arm. The problem of what to do with her was one that he was still putting off, and the need for speed left no time for argument. Chevalier frowned as he saw that the woman was coming with them, but he made no comment.

With Powell leading the way they ran swiftly across the airfield. The plane was a four-seater and Larren and the woman scrambled into the seats behind the pilot. Chevalier sat beside Powell, and the boy Hamid hurried to pull the chocks away from the wheels. Powell started the engine and warmed her up as the young man ran clear, and then he started to taxi towards the end of the field. He turned her so that he had the whole length for take-off and increased the speed.

"She'll bump," he said warningly. "But that's only because she's a slight plane. Once she's actually aloft it's smoother than riding in a bus."

The remark was directed at Barbara, and was probably a routine reassurance for all non-flyers that he took in the air. The woman showed no sign that she had heard, and now seemed resigned to anything that fate might have in store for her. Powell gave her a puzzled glance, and then concentrated on taking the plane off the ground.

The grassy earth was now rushing dizzily below them, and the sound of the engine was a singing roar. The wheels lifted, then bumped down again, then lifted a second time as the Argus soared upwards. She swayed to one side, the left wing dipping earthwards, but Powell was grinning happily as he levelled her out and started to climb. To their right lay a magnificent aerial view of Tangier, and the gold-fringed bay where a large ferry boat slowly made her way out into the straits towards Algeciras.

"Now," Powell said cheerfully. "Supposing you erks tell me where I'm supposed to be flying this thing. At least tell me that."

Larren smiled, although he was already filled with a sense of failure. The homing signal from his receiver had started to fade swiftly before they had reached Tangier, and now it was wholly dead. He could only give the last reading on the finder needle and hope.

"Inland," he said. "Fly due south-east. And give her maximum speed."

Powell looked back at him dubiously, but he obeyed without asking any questions. At least, Larren thought, he wasn't one of those Englishmen who had to be introduced before taking any action. The pilot brought the Argus on to the desired course, then put on a pair of dark glasses to protect his eyes as he settled down to fly.

Chevalier took on the job of explaining everything that had happened, and why they needed to catch up with the Piper Cherokee that must be somewhere in the blazing blue bowl of the sky ahead. Powell's face became more serious as he realised that he was pursuing two killers, and he turned with a word of genuine sympathy for Barbara Mallory. She did not respond, but stared silently out of the window.

They flew over the spot where they had first seen the enemy aircraft, but now the grassy bowl was empty and even the large American convertible had vanished. Larren's unsmiling mouth tightened as they flew on, and there was still no signal from the homing receiver. The sky ahead was empty, and the earth below a rugged pattern of green and sun-baked brown, reminiscent of Spain but without the endless olive groves. Chevalier reached the end of his explaining and Larren asked, "What are our chances of picking up that other plane?"

Powell frowned. "Evens, I reckon. Planes are not like cars, restricted to roads and liable to turn corners. If she started off by flying due south-east then she'll probably continue that way. What really counts is her speed. A Cherokee is much faster than this crate, and if she's in a hurry then we haven't a hope of getting near her. But if she's cruising and taking her time, and I stay flat out —" he shrugged — "well, I just might catch up to her. How far ahead do you reckon she is?"

"About twenty-five minutes," Chevalier supplied. "No more."

"It's plenty."

"You don't have to catch the plane," Larren reminded him. "Just get within signal range of that transmitter they're carrying, and then hold back."

They flew on for the next half-hour, bypassing the town of Tetouan some thirty miles south of Tangier. With every mile Larren's hopes dwindled, and at every moment he expected Powell to shrug and say that the chase was pointless. But Powell kept going, pushing the old Argus to its limit. Chevalier for once had lost his natural gaiety and sat tensely by the pilot, while Barbara continued to stare dully at the broad-winged shadow of the plane that kept pace directly below. And then suddenly the receiver that Larren held close to his ear began very faintly to bleep.

"We've got them," he said thankfully, and the two men in the front of the cockpit both looked round and smiled. Chevalier's face was a beam, and Powell looked relieved.

"It's just as well," the pilot said. "Much more of this flat-out flying and she would have vibrated herself to bits." He throttled the Argus down slightly and asked, "What course?"

The direction finder was registering again, and Larren answered promptly, "They're veering more to the east. Bring her nose round, and I'll tell you when."

Powell obliged, banking the plane slowly to the left.

"That'll do," Larren said. "They're directly ahead again."

Powell nodded, and reduced the speed of the Argus a little more so that the bleeping signal from the receiver was again only just audible. There was no sign of the tiny red-and-white

Cherokee in the glaring blue waste of the sky ahead, but they did not need to see it. They knew it was there.

For the next three hours they droned on, with the sun getting lower behind them, and their accompanying shadow racing farther ahead. They crossed the jagged range of the Atlas Mountains, flying high above thrusting peaks, their lower slopes wildly tangled with pines and olives and struggling young oaks, mixed with flanks of rough grey crags and slashes of red soil. The violent beauty roused Barbara slightly from her lethargy of grief and despair, but she still made no conversation. She knew now that Larren had not killed her father, but she also knew that he had known what was to happen and had not lifted a finger to save him. Larren knew that she might hold part of the answers to more questions, but he could not bring himself to interrogate her again, at least not yet.

The mountains passed slowly behind them, and gradually the land became more and more desert. The souks and kasbahs, tiny jumbles of brown or grey-white, block-shaped houses, clustered around trees or date palms, became fewer and fewer, giving up their advance into the wastes of yellow sand. The Argus flew on into the silent, waiting Sahara, and still the homing signal bleeped faintly to show that the Cherokee was still somewhere in the emptiness beyond their whirling propeller. Powell was beginning to look concerned, and at last he broke the long silence that had enveloped them.

"It looks as though our friends are heading right on into Algeria," he said. "And I'll be in trouble if I start crossing frontiers. In any case, I'm nearly at my limit if I'm going to turn round and make it back to my own base."

Larren grimaced and then said, "As long as you don't get beyond range of the nearest airport where you can refuel, does it really matter?"

Powell looked back and said wryly, "Chum, you don't just drop into any airport you happen to be passing. There are rules and regulations about such things, and I'm only supposed to be flying pleasure flights over Tangier Bay."

"I know," Larren admitted. "But Jacques told you why this flight is so important. That plane ahead belongs to an organisation that calls itself the A.F.P., the organisation that planned the assassination of the Prime Minister of England. That's why we have to track it back to its base."

"Okay," Powell said. "Don't accuse me of being unpatriotic. I just thought you ought to know the score. If I do cross the frontier and have to use another airfield then there'll be a stink, and you'll be in it. And according to the storybooks you secret service Johnnies, or whatever it is you are, don't like to make yourselves that noticeable."

Larren noticed that Powell made no mention of the fact that his flying licence, and consequently his living, might also be in jeopardy, and he felt a new respect for the ginger-headed pilot. He said quietly, "In this case I think any risk is worth taking. We don't know what else these people may have got planned, and if we lose them now we may never get close enough again to stop them."

Powell shrugged. "Spit in my eye and call me stupid," he said resignedly. "We'll fly as far as possible."

There was nothing below them now but sand dunes rippling away to the scorching rim of the world. There was no life, and nothing moved but the undulating shadow of the Argus as it wriggled steadily across the gentle slopes and valleys. The sun was low and a long way behind them, but the heat was still sticky and oppressive. The drone of their engine was the only sound above the barely noticeable bleep of the homer.

They flew on for another half-hour before Powell broke the silence again and said, "I calculate that we're now leaving Morocco. Our destination is definitely in Algeria."

Larren was thoughtful. "It could add up. Jouvert, one of the men we caught in England, had an Algerian background. We know that he served out here with the French Foreign Legion, but we don't know exactly when or where."

No one seemed to think that worth a comment, and they relapsed into silence again. There was nothing below them to show that they had crossed a frontier, and the desert continued as before, an empty waste of endless sand.

Another hour of flying passed slowly, and another hundred miles of desert unrolled like a blank, yellowed film below them. Then Chevalier said, "Gerry, how much fuel have we got left?"

"Enough for about another two hundred and fifty miles, but only for another hundred if I'm going to turn back and make a Moroccan airfield."

Larren said grimly, "I didn't expect them to be flying as far as this. What's the maximum range of that Cherokee?"

"About seven hundred," Powell answered him. "A little less than this in fact. But if he's going the full distance and then lands somewhere that's going to be unfriendly to us, then we're buggered."

Chevalier scowled, an unusual expression for him and one which ultimately meant that he was thinking. He said slowly, "If that is so, then the Cherokee must have refuelled somewhere close to Tangier before picking up those two men. That fact might help us to find them even if we are forced to turn back."

"Could have been Quezzane," Powell said, "or Tetouan, or even Tangier itself. All depends on —"

"Forget it!" Larren cut in sharply. "I think this is it."

Powell and Chevalier both twisted to face him, and then looked down at the homing receiver in his hands. The signal was bleeping strongly and growing louder every second.

"They've landed all right." Powell turned quickly back to the controls and cut the throttles. Their airspeed dropped and he took the Argus low towards the earth. The violent bleeping increased and Larren had to tune down the volume. The Argus skimmed along at an altitude of fifty feet, and all three men stared rigidly forward.

"There!" Powell snapped the word briskly, and immediately banked the plane away to the left. Larren had a fleeting glimpse of some scattered buildings on the horizon, and the tiny red-and-white toy that was the Cherokee standing among them. Then they were behind the Argus and Powell had completed his turn, taking them back along their own route.

"I don't think they could have spotted us," he said over his shoulder. "So what do we do now?"

"Circle round," Larren said flatly. "There were some hills to the left of those buildings and if we approach low we should be able to land behind them without being seen. We'll wait till the sun goes down, and then I'm going to talk a walk over there and find out just what the hell is going on."

CHAPTER 13: THE SCIMITAR

Powell was not happy with the idea of putting the Argus down for a landing, and his misgivings were obvious as he swung the plane round to survey the terrain. His casual attitude had hardened, and he sat more grimly at the controls. The desert wheeled below them as he made a wide circling turn that brought them behind the low red hills that Larren had pointed out, and then he throttled down again to make a low approach.

The hills loomed close in a barrier of harsh red stone, scoured by the erosive force of a thousand sandstorms. The pitted crags were bleak and hostile, but immediately around them was a stretch of hard ground, scattered with stones and boulders. It was like the solid beach of an island, isolated in the vast sea of unbroken dunes. Powell flew over the hard strip, his gaze concentrated in search of a place to land, and then he banked away once more and headed back into the desert.

"It might be possible," he said dubiously. "I can pick a landing path that will avoid the biggest of those rocks down there. But even a small one could throw us over, and although it looks hard enough there could be soft spots of sand." He looked back and added bluntly, "I wouldn't try it for pleasure — or for money."

Larren said slowly, "You know the risks, and you know the reason. It has to be your decision."

Powell smiled thinly. "Typical buck-passer; you must have come from Whitehall." He looked at Chevalier. "Jacques, it's your neck as well. What do you think?"

Chevalier leaned back in his seat, tilting his flat vaudeville hat away from his eyes. He said simply, "Gerry, I have implicit faith in your skill and judgement. If you tried to land on the hump of a wobbly camel I would come along for the ride."

"So that makes two suicide types." Powell turned his head again. "That only leaves you, Miss. What's your reaction?"

Barbara Mallory stared at him blankly, as though she had not quite grasped the situation around her, and then she broke her long silence and said quietly, "I don't care, Mr Powell. Those men killed my father while Larren and his friend simply stood by and let it happen. If you land and they go after those killers, then perhaps they'll all kill each other. I think I'd like to see that."

Powell grimaced. "Two suicides and one don't care. The company I keep!" He banked the Argus and flew back again towards the range of red hills.

For the second time the plane swept low over the proposed landing area, with Powell leaning forward and sideways to peer through the cabin window. He did not look any happier as he studied the ground below, but as he banked the plane for another retreat, he said grimly, "This is it. Next time round I'll put her down for a landing. And let's hope that Allah the All-Merciful has a little left over for an unbeliever."

Nobody answered him, and he brought the Argus round slowly and gently for the final approach. The barrier of red rock rushed towards them, and then he cut down on the throttles and swung the plane round for the last time. The bare earth rose to meet them as the red hills flashed past their wingtip, and Powell's face was a rigid mask as he pushed on the joystick. Chevalier sat equally tense, and Larren could feel the sweat breaking out on the back of his neck and the palms of his hands. Barbara had closed her eyes tightly and her head was bowed forward, but Larren could feel a stiffness in her body that told that she was not wholly resigned.

The Argus touched down, her wheels bumping and spinning before settling on to solid ground. Dirt and stones spattered against the underside of the fuselage and the tyres screamed. The whole aircraft lurched and threw them forward, and Powell's lips peeled back ferociously from his teeth as he fought the bucking controls. There was another jolt as the tailwheel struck earth, and then the whole plane was rocking wildly as she slithered forward. A scattering of heavy stones caused her to bounce and yaw crazily, balancing on one wheel, and for a moment Larren thought that a crash was inevitable. He twisted in his seat, crushing Barbara's face close to his chest in an instinctive effort to shield her, but somehow Powell pulled the plane back on to an even keel and held her upright. Her speed was decreasing now and he steered a better course in the last few moments before she rolled to a final stop, still upright, and still in one piece.

Powell's hand remained steady as he reached out to shut off the engines, but it trembled slightly as he withdrew. He leaned back in his seat and his body sagged weakly as he closed his eyes. The engines died into silence as the dust settled behind them, and the old Fairchild Argus stood perfectly still. Simon Larren could feel a dryness in his throat, and it was not until Barbara tried to move beneath him that he realised that her face was still jammed against his chest. He eased his body away from her in time to prevent her complete suffocation, and her feeble coughing made the first sound. She looked at him hesitantly, but the hostility was still inside her. She turned her face away and continued to cough.

Chevalier was the first to speak. "An excellent landing," he said. "All we want now is for the pretty hostess to bring round the orange juice and coffee."

Powell opened his eyes. "Sorry, Jacques. This is one airline that doesn't measure up to B.O.A.C. standards." He smiled briefly and reached for the door. "Let's get down and stretch our legs. I feel like a cramped sardine."

One by one they climbed down from the plane, standing in the shadow of the high wing and looking out towards the red hills less than a hundred yards away. Barbara was the last to climb down, but she did so after a long moment of hesitation.

Larren was already calculating the best route of climbing the rocky barrier, and after a moment he turned to Powell. "How far would you say we were from the spot where that Cherokee landed?"

Powell frowned. "Six or seven miles, I reckon. That's after we've crossed this lot."

Larren squinted towards the red ball of the sun hanging low on the western skyline. "It'll be dark long before we get there," he said. "We might as well start now. If Jacques and I don't get back before dawn you'd better take off without us and report what's happened."

"Hold on now," Powell said. "Jacques and I have an understanding. If I help him out then I usually get to share in the fun. Besides, it looks to me as though that Cherokee landed on a genuine airstrip. One of those buildings looked like a control tower. And if I'm right you might need me. Airplanes and airfields are my business."

Larren smiled, for he had expected nothing less. "All right," he said. "We'll be glad of your help. But you'd better tune the radio in the Argus, and show Miss Mallory how to use it before we leave. Then if the three of us fail to get back she can call up some help."

Powell nodded and turned to the woman. "How about it?" he asked. "Can you operate the radio if I show you what to do?"

Barbara looked at him, and then nodded slowly. Powell smiled at her in encouragement and then helped her to climb back into the cockpit of the plane. He followed her in and started to explain the dials and call signs while Larren waited with Chevalier in the shade of the wing.

After a few moments the pilot rejoined them again, pulling on the leather jacket that had lain beside him throughout the flight. Larren fished in his pocket and then offered him the black-nosed automatic.

"You'd better take this," he said, "just in case it proves to be a lively night. Jacques and I already have one. This belonged to Miss Mallory."

Powell looked at it. "Then you'd best give it back to Miss Mallory," he advised. "It might make her mind easier if she's got to spend all night sitting alone in the desert. Besides —" he balled a big-knuckled fist and grinned — "I'm pretty capable with this. If there's any shooting I'll leave it to you experts."

Larren hesitated, and then turned towards the plane where Barbara still sat silently in the cabin. He held the gun out towards her. "I don't think you'll have any cause to use it," he assured her, "but keep it handy just in case."

She stared at him uncertainly, and the dying sun beamed red lights through her long auburn hair. Her eyes were wide and steady, and for a moment the likeness to Andrea was again strong. Larren's composure cracked a little from the inside, and he felt a bitter resentment at the chain of circumstances that had built up her enmity against him. Then she reached for the automatic and placed it on the seat beside her. She looked over his head and spoke to Powell. "I'll be all right." Her voice was quiet but level. "I'll wait until tomorrow morning, and if you're not back by then I'll make the radio call like you showed me. Don't worry about me."

Powell nodded and smiled at her, and Simon Larren turned slowly away. The three men moved off together towards the red hills, and Barbara Mallory watched them go. Then she looked down at the automatic on the seat beside her. She remembered her father anxiously insisting that she should have it, and suddenly there was an uncontrollable relief at being alone. At last she could really cry.

It took the three men less than twenty minutes to reach the top of the rocky barrier, and by then the sun had sunk below the rim of the world and faint starlight illuminated their path. Chevalier was panting slightly, but neither Larren nor Powell were affected by the climb. Below them the rock-strewn hill slope tumbled down again towards the desert. They could see nothing across the darkened waste, but Larren had brought the homing receiver and once more it was picking up its bleeping signal.

They paused only to check their direction and then began the descent, Larren leading with Powell close behind, and Chevalier bringing up the rear. They moved faster now, and it took them no more than ten minutes to reach the desert floor. Again there was a strip of hard, stony ground, but it stretched only a short distance and they soon found themselves sinking into soft sand. Their pace slowed again as they floundered forward, and ahead there was nothing but low empty dunes.

They marched on for the next two hours. The night became colder, the stars became brighter, and the once-golden desert took on a faint, silvery sheen that made the sloping dunes and the wind-rippled sand look even more like some vast petrified sea. The homing signal led them unerringly in a direct line towards its parent transmitter, but Powell constantly checked their direction with the stars, his navigator's mind reminding him that there would be no signal to help them return to the plane.

They walked in silence except for an occasional curse as one of them slipped or stumbled, and Larren gradually tuned down the homing receiver as its heightened signal indicated that they were nearing the end of their trek. All three were fit, capable men and although the dragging sand had a tiring effect on their leg muscles they made good time. Only Chevalier, who was shorter and slighter than the two Englishmen, showed any signs of heavy breathing. The distance was less than Powell had first anticipated, and after crossing some four and a half miles of desert they climbed up the slope of a high dune and saw the outlines of buildings less than half a mile below them.

They rested for a moment, and then continued more cautiously. The buildings drew closer, and soon the clear starlight showed that Powell's guess had been correct. They were approaching a properly constructed airstrip. The pilot pointed out the control tower that dominated the few smaller buildings around it, and the larger shapes of two square black hangars more to the left.

Larren frowned and said softly, "But why would anyone want to build an airstrip out here?"

Powell halted for a minute and pushed back his peaked cap with one finger. "I'd say it was abandoned," he hazarded. "Before the present occupants started using it, I mean. If you look over to the right you can see an old skeleton pylon. It probably supported a radar bowl at one time, but there's nothing there now. It could be a wartime relic, left over from the North African campaigns — or possibly it was abandoned by the French when they pulled out and gave Algeria her independence."

They were silent for a moment, and then slowly they moved on again. In unspoken agreement they veered to the left to place another dune between them and the airstrip, and then warily climbed the slope. They lay on their stomachs in the sand when they reached the top, and from here they were able to look down on the long concrete strip of the runway that lay beyond the buildings. Powell again pushed back his cap, rubbing a forefinger thoughtfully into his unruly ginger hair.

"Now what do you make of that?" he mused. "That runway has definitely been lengthened recently; you can see where the fresh concrete starts. But why? They certainly don't need that extra length to land a poky little Piper Cherokee — so what do they expect to land here?"

"Let us go closer," Chevalier suggested. "Perhaps we can find out."

Larren nodded in agreement, and one by one they slid down the far side of the dune. The sharp starlight was a danger to them now and they kept as low as possible as they closed in upon the silent airstrip, crouching where the dunes helped to conceal them, and wriggling on elbows and knees where there was no cover at all. They approached to within a hundred yards of the nearest building, and then Larren checked their advance. He had switched off the homing receiver now that it had served its purpose, and slipped it into his pocket, and now the starlight glinted dully on the Smith & Wesson in his hand.

He said softly, "We'll check those two big hangars first. I'm curious to see what's inside. You'd better stay here, Jacques, and then you can cover us if anything goes wrong."

Chevalier nodded. He was puffing again from the exertion of scrambling across the sand, and he accepted that he was the slowest of the three. He was also professional enough to know the wisdom of leaving one man in reserve. He smiled and said, "Be careful, my friends. This is not Tangier where I can call upon a score of my contacts, and alone even Jacques Chevalier has his limitations."

"Then we'll try not to stir up a hornet's nest," Larren promised.

He looked at Powell and received a brief nod, then together they ran low towards the nearest of the two large hangars. Chevalier watched them go, then took a small automatic from his pocket and checked it calmly as he settled down to recover his breath and wait.

Larren and Powell had to cover the last fifty yards to the hangar on their stomachs, worming forward like slithering snakes, and to their surprise they found that it was unguarded. They stood up once they had gained the patch of shadow against the hangar wall, and with Larren leading moved swiftly but silently towards the closed doors. There was no sound from inside, and again to his surprise Larren found that the small side door was unlocked. He eased his body inside and Powell followed him into the unrelieved darkness. They closed the door behind them and listened for a moment, then Larren produced the small pencil torch that was part of his standard equipment.

He flashed the thin but powerful beam of light slowly around the great hangar, and after a few moments found the sleek red-and-white lines of the Piper Cherokee. The smart little four-seater stood in the centre of the floor, facing the doors and ready to be rolled out on to the runway. He explored farther, but the beam showed nothing else but workbenches lining the walls and some stacked oil drums.

"Let's try the next one," Powell murmured.

Larren nodded and switched off the torch. They left the hangar and carefully closed the door behind them, then crouched low and dashed across to the front of the second hangar fifty yards away. Again they halted in shadow with their backs against the wall, but still there was nothing to alarm them, and after a moment Larren turned his attention to the door. This time a padlock barred the way.

Larren grimaced and handed his Smith & Wesson to Powell. Then, from the hidden sheath inside his jacket, he drew the flat throwing knife, and with its point he set to work on the screws holding the padlock bracket. They were stiff and difficult to remove, especially as he was trying not to leave any tell-tale scratches that would show up after they had been replaced. However, the wood of the door jamb was half rotten, and once the screws did start to turn they came out more easily. The job took several minutes, but at last the bracket came away, dangling uselessly from the padlock, and Larren was able to open the door.

Powell followed him inside once again, and for the second time Larren used the slender beam from his torch. Almost immediately it found a second aircraft, but this was no private toy. The smooth rounded nose was twice as high as the Cherokee, and the hollow bulge of powerful jet intakes fitted snugly to each side of the fuselage. The wings were swept sharply back, giving her a poised appearance, as though straining to leap forward. Larren heard Powell suck in a sharp, startled breath, and for a moment neither of them spoke. Larren continued to move the torch slowly back and forth, picking out the British roundels and Royal Navy markings on their unexpected find. And then he too felt a moment of qualm as the beam settled on one of the two ten-foot-long rocket missiles slung close to the fuselage under the wings.

Powell said in a hushed voice, "She's a naval strike-fighter. A Vickers Supermarine Scimitar. And those ugly little brutes tucked close against her belly are Bullpup air-to-surface missiles with a high-explosive warhead. But what in merry hell is she doing here?"

Larren had no answer to that, but even if he had there would have been no time for him to give it. For in that moment every light suddenly flashed on in the great hangar, and a sardonic voice behind them said calmly, "She's minding her own business, old chap. But what is more to the point is, what in merry hell are *you* doing here?"

CHAPTER 14: THE MAN FROM ZURICH

Larren swivelled on his left heel, the knife in his hand automatically flipping to a throwing position between his fingers. The move was instinctive, but just as quickly he let the poised blade drop from his hand and clatter to the concrete floor of the hangar. Powell twisted almost as fast with the Smith & Wesson clamped in his big fist, but he too had the sense to drop it. Both of them raised their hands slowly above their heads.

The man who had addressed them was young and very smooth-faced. He was about five foot seven tall and almost girlishly slender. His teeth were perfectly white and even and there were faint freckles across the bridge of his nose. He was smiling, but the smile was no more than a polite fixture on his face, and his pale blue eyes had an alert sharpness. He wore the smart navy-blue uniform of the Fleet Air Arm, with pilot's wings and the single gold rings of a sub-lieutenant on his sleeves. However, the large black Luger in his hand was not naval issue, and neither were the three men crowding behind his back with skeleton-handled machine pistols naval personnel.

Larren said slowly, "And who might you be?"

The man in uniform widened his smile. "My name is Goodhart — Sub-Lieutenant Peter Goodhart. And that's my personal aircraft that you've been admiring. And now that I've told you that, it's your turn to answer my question. Who are you?"

Larren said nothing; instead he silently weighed up the man in front of him. Goodhart's tone, and the pride with which he had uttered his own name, had betrayed him as another self-loving egoist, but this time there was no sign of the cheerful nature that had redeemed that same trait in Jacques Chevalier. Goodhart held himself in high esteem, but he had no warmth for the world, and only contempt showed behind his smile.

Powell made no attempt to answer either. He had half turned his head to look back at the Scimitar now that she was fully revealed, and his trained eye noticed every detail. He said slowly, "External fuel tanks, enough to give her maximum range. That's about one thousand five hundred miles, isn't it, Goodhart? And two Bullpups, radio-controlled, if I remember rightly, with a range of something over two miles once they leave the aircraft. That's a pretty lethal combination. What do you intend to do with it?"

Goodhart said pleasantly, "You sound like a pilot — look like one too in that leather jacket. So one must presume that you came by plane. Where is it? And what led you to this airfield?"

Both Larren and Powell remained silent. The three men behind Goodhart had spread themselves out and moved closer with their machine pistols levelled. Two of them were local men in knitted skull caps and soiled djellabas, their bare toes protruding through old sandals, but the third was a heavy crop-headed man in a windcheater jacket and dark trousers. His face was dark, showing Mediterranean origin. He said harshly, "They won't talk until they're made to — but I think we can manage that all right."

Goodhart looked at him almost condescendingly. "This is Borrelli," he said. "He's area controller here. He's a nice fellow once you get to know him."

Goodhart's tone insinuated that Borrelli was not a nice fellow at all, but although the big man's lips tightened he made no retort. Larren knew then that for some reason Goodhart had to be humoured, for Borrelli did not look the sort of man who would normally take an insult without response.

Borrelli said flatly, "You two, put your hands upon your heads and keep them there. Aziz, pick up the knife and that gun."

Larren and Powell did as they were told, and one of the two men came cautiously forward to pick up their weapons. Afterwards there was silence. Goodhart asked no more questions, and both he and Borrelli seemed to be waiting for something. Then suddenly there came the sharp sound of distant gunfire, a single bark from an automatic followed by a quick stutter from a machine pistol. As the noise died away Goodhart's eyes gleamed with malicious satisfaction.

"I think," he said, "that our friends have just collected your friend. Perhaps you were hoping that he would help you, but unfortunately you were spotted before you separated. We delayed in picking you up to give our second party time to circle round the man you left behind. We didn't want him to take flight if we inadvertently created a battle out of your apprehension."

"Clever little mummy's boy," Powell said bitterly.

Goodhart stared at him, and the poised self-confidence seemed to peel away from him as the taunt struck home. His face stiffened, and for a moment Larren thought that Powell had earned himself a heavy bullet from the black Luger.

Then Borrelli said sharply, "Enough of this. Aziz, lead the way outside. You gentlemen will follow him, and remember that you have no chance of escape. You both have broad backs that make excellent close-range targets."

The man named Aziz nodded obediently and turned away. The remaining man and Borrelli moved to one side, and after a moment of hesitation Goodhart joined them. Larren and Powell had no choice but to follow Aziz out of the hangar. As they passed through the door Larren murmured softly, "Go easy, Gerry. Mummy's boy can be dangerous."

Powell's head inclined slightly in acknowledgement, but he didn't answer. Aziz was standing well back from the door and covering them with the machine pistol, and they were forced to wait until the remaining three men had followed them into the open. There was a delay while Borrelli switched off the lights in the hangar and closed the door, and then the two captives were marched across the empty stretch of sand towards the airport buildings.

Another party of armed men converged to meet them from the desert, and in the middle was the unmistakable figure of Chevalier. The little Frenchman had lost his jaunty straw hat and his face was tight-lipped as he held his left arm close against his chest. A guard flanked him on either side, and as the two parties closed up Larren saw that behind him were the two men they had trailed from Tangier: Henry Mallory's killers.

"I am sorry, my friends." Chevalier's face twisted wryly. "It would appear that I have let you down."

Behind them Borrelli gave a grating chuckle. "You most certainly have, friend." He paused and then added, "Nice work, Ricard. You and Hassim make a good team."

The two killers smiled politely.

There was no more conversation as the two parties fell into step and headed for a large lighted building beside the control tower. Larren and his two companions were herded inside, and Larren guessed from the raised platform at the far end of the room that it had once been used for lectures and briefings.

Now it had been adapted into a form of community centre, with assorted chairs and tables and a scattering of magazines, books and ashtrays.

The prisoners were halted in the centre of the floor and turned round slowly, Larren and Powell still holding their hands on their heads. Borrelli had seated himself with one haunch on the edge of a table and now allowed his machine pistol to relax. Hassim and Ricard stood attentively to one side, like polite, deadly twins, each with his right hand in the jacket pocket of their casually cut suits. Goodhart stood alone, toying with his Luger and looking slightly petulant, while the other men spread themselves out and waited.

Borrelli's swarthy face cracked thinly, the nearest he would ever get to a smile. "Aziz," he ordered, "go and inform Mr Khalil that everything is under control, and that we have now picked up three strangers who were prying round the hangars. I think that he may wish to be present at their interrogation."

Aziz nodded silently, and backed out of the room. No one spoke after he had left, and Goodhart nonchalantly found himself an armchair and reclined lazily. Powell looked at the dark stains seeping beneath Chevalier's fingers and spreading down the pale grey sleeve of his jacket, and finally demanded, "While we're waiting, can't you do something for that arm?"

"We might," Borrelli said. "In time we might try twisting it."

Powell stiffened angrily and Larren gave him a warning look. It wasn't going to help them if the ginger-headed pilot lost his temper. Powell still looked mad enough to start hitting out regardlessly with his fists.

Larren looked at Goodhart in an effort to change the situation. "It must have taken some clever thinking to acquire a fast strike-fighter like the Scimitar. How did you do it?" He smiled and added, "I'm assuming, of course, that you are responsible for its being here."

"Quite right, old chap. I am responsible. I simply stole the thing." Goodhart was smiling now that he was back in the limelight again. "You see, I had reached the conclusion that the Scimitar would be serving a far more desirable purpose with the A.F.P. than with the Royal Navy."

"Yes," Larren prompted, "but how did you manage it?"

Borrelli glowered. "Stop asking questions, mister. You already know too much."

"Oh, do shut up, Borrelli!" Goodhart was nettled by the interruption to his moment of self-idolatry, and careless of the other's authority. "Now that they've actually seen the plane the damage has been done. It doesn't matter now if they hear how we pulled it off." He looked back at Larren and asked, "Do you remember the Scimitar that blew up on a routine training flight just over six months ago? It caused quite a mystery because no one could explain why it should have blown up, and as the explosion took place over deep water they were never able to examine any of the wreckage."

Larren remembered vaguely, but Powell's attention was fully claimed now and it was the pilot who answered. "I heard of it," he said. "The plane took off from a carrier doing some tactical exercises in the Atlantic, somewhere north of the Canaries. They were tracking her by radar back on the parent ship until she reached the turning point of her flight. Then she vanished for a moment, reappeared, and then apparently blew up."

Goodhart nodded smugly. "That's how it appeared on the radar screens back on the carrier, but that's not exactly how it happened. That Scimitar was the same one that's now resting in the hangar out there, and I was the pilot. What they actually saw exploding on their radar screens was nothing but an old

Avro Anson that we managed to buy up quite cheaply." He chuckled and explained, "It was all planned well in advance. In fact, we had to wait for months until the carrier was operating in waters where our scheme was possible. It's no simple task to arrange a short notice rendezvous between two planes of vastly different speeds and capabilities. However, we had one stroke of luck, my briefing for that last flight took place several hours before take-off, so I had plenty of time to radio our people ashore, just a simple code-word to go ahead and the location of the rendezvous. After that I jettisoned the transmitter they had given me just in case the call had been picked up aboard the carrier. The old Annie had been standing by at Safi airfield on the Atlantic coast of Morocco for the past week, ostensibly with engine trouble, and she took off several hours before I did in order to time her arrival with mine.

"When I reached the turning point of my flight the Annie was there below me, exactly as planned, cruising along just above the wave tops and below the level of the carrier's radar. She started to climb and I dived the Scimitar down to sea level behind her. That's where the carrier lost me for a minute, and when they thought they had picked me up again the new blip on their screens was actually the old Annie. The Annie blew up, while I raced the Scimitar away below radar level until I neared the African coast. Then I climbed to fifty thousand feet and brought her here."

Larren and Powell had listened in silence, and now Powell said slowly, "What happened to the pilot of the Anson?"

Goodhart shrugged. "That was sad. He thought he had three minutes between pressing the switch and the big blast, just enough time to bale out. He thought too that there was going to be a seaplane stooging around below radar level to pick him up, but of course there was no seaplane and the explosion was instantaneous."

Powell stared down at the lounging man in naval uniform, disgust mirrored in his eyes. There was no sign now of his original happy-go-lucky attitude, and again he showed signs of a hot temper nearing eruption. Larren saw the danger and cut in swiftly.

"But what about the Anson? She must have been expected somewhere after she took off from Safi. How did you explain her disappearance?"

"I told you, everything was very well planned." Goodhart crossed his legs as he spoke and calmly rested the Luger on his knee. "There was a second Anson here at this airfield. She couldn't have made the rendezvous, of course — she hadn't the range — but she could and did fly to Tangier, where the first Anson was expected. She had identical registration markings to the decoy we blew up, and as far as I know she's still flying in the decoy's place. So you see, there was no disappearance to explain. The people who planned this operation have unlimited supplies of cash and resources, and they've planned to cover every possible angle. Even I don't know every detail that went into the overall plan, but it's worked perfectly, and the Navy have no suspicion that I might be alive, or that the Scimitar might be in one piece. They believe that we're both scattered in tiny pieces over the seabed of the Atlantic."

"I think I understand," Larren assured him. "But why was it done? Why do the A.F.P. need the Scimitar? And why did you take the colossal risk of helping them?"

Goodhart smiled. "That, old chap, is something that you don't need to know."

Larren hesitated, wondering whether he could play on the young man's vanity any farther. But then he saw the watchful look in Borrelli's eyes and knew that it was not worth the risk. Borrelli had humoured Goodhart because so far it did not matter, but if the young pilot attempted to go beyond past history and into future intentions then Borrelli would intervene.

Then Larren's deliberations became irrelevant, for the outer door opened and Aziz reappeared, and with him was a tall, hook-nosed man in an immaculate white suit. His arms were long and the cuffs of his white silk shirt were fastened with heavy gold links, while at his throat he wore a narrow, gold-coloured bow tie. His hair was black and crinkly and his eyes were dark and brilliant. His mouth was a sharp line below the hooked nose.

Khalil had flown out from Zurich two days ago to take complete control of the last stages of the operation on behalf of Raab and his colleagues. There was a moment of respectful silence, and Larren knew that at last he was face to face with one of the leaders of this mysterious organisation which so far he knew only by its initials. He watched the hard, cruel face and knew also that here was a man of both power and wealth. The reverence in which he was held proved his power, and only a man who could afford to discard his suits daily would wear one that was pure white.

Borrelli had straightened up from his table and moved aside, and after a moment even Goodhart rose awkwardly to his feet. Khalil ignored them and stared at each of the three prisoners in turn, then he switched his gaze to Borrelli. His voice was calm and betrayed no hint of feeling, but there was an underlying note that made it clear that he would not speak with anyone lower than the area controller.

"Have they talked yet?"

Borrelli shook his head. "Not yet, Mr Khalil. But so far we haven't used any kind of persuasion."

Khalil looked at them again, his gaze ranging from Chevalier to Powell, and finally to Larren. Neither his tone nor his expression changed as he said simply, "Kill them."

Borrelli stared.

Khalil lifted his arm and pointed to all three in turn. "Kill them," he repeated coldly. "Here and now."

Borrelli hesitated another second, and then he nodded. He lifted the machine pistol that had dangled against his thigh, and held the skeleton handle against his hip as he gripped it with both hands. The room vibrated as the first burst hit Chevalier, and then the second struck Powell as he attempted to move. The two men crumpled to the floor, and Borrelli's face was shining with sweat as he swung the pistol towards Simon Larren.

CHAPTER 15: MASS MURDER

"Stop!"

Khalil snapped the command as Borrelli's finger was tightening to fire the final burst, and slowly the big dark-faced man lowered his gun. He turned and looked back at the white-suited Man with bewilderment showing on his face.

"But, Mr Khalil — you said —"

"I know what I said. Now I am countermanding the order." Khalil looked down at the two bodies, and then glanced up again into Larren's pale face. He said, "There is nothing more finely calculated to shatter a man's resistance than to brutally destroy his friends in front of him. Show him a foretaste of his own death in the same moment — pluck him back from the edge of eternity, in fact — and the shock will weaken him even more. As you so rightly assumed, Borrelli, I want to know how and why these men came here. But we only need one of them to talk, and I think that now our lone survivor will co-operate."

Larren said nothing. He looked down at the two men at his feet, a stunned sickness in his heart. Chevalier had twisted round, fallen, and then rolled on to his back. Now his body was still and his cream shirt-front was soaked with red. His eyes were open and there was still surprise and horror in them at the sudden violence of his death. Powell had fallen across the Frenchman's feet, his mouth gritted in agony and his hands clasped across his stomach. His peaked cap had rolled away from his wild ginger hair, and despite his big body he still looked as though he had been cut down in his boyhood.

Larren stared at their dead faces and felt the sickness inside him harden. They had been two damned good men. He had known neither of them for long, but each had possessed his own brand of cheerful confidence that had made them immediate friends. And now, in the short space of seconds, they were nothing but empty, lifeless shells.

The first shock had passed now, for Larren had lived a lifetime of violent episodes, and the sickness in his heart became cold, controlled fury. It was as well that neither Khalil nor Borrelli looked directly into his eyes in that moment. If they had, and could have read what they saw there, then they would have killed him too on the spot.

Slowly Larren looked back to face Khalil, but now the promise of atonement no longer reflected in his grey-green gaze. For the moment the other side held all the cards and Larren waited.

Khalil looked at Borrelli. "Go ahead. You may now interrogate him."

Borrelli shifted forward, standing splay-legged and pointing the machine pistol at Larren's middle. "All right, mister. For a start you can tell us who you are and how you came to be here."

Larren was sweating and he knew that his face was still pale. He said quietly, "I don't seem to remember. I think I must have had a nasty shock. They sometimes bring on amnesia."

Borrelli stared at him, and behind the big man's back Larren saw Khalil silently raise his eyebrows. Then Borrelli said sharply, "Search him — and search those two bodies. It may save us some time."

He stepped back, and Aziz and another man stepped forward to rifle through Larren's pockets. Two others crouched over the bodies on the floor. They threw their finds on the table and Borrelli checked them over.

"A driving licence," he said, "made out in the name of Jacques Chevalier and giving a Tangier address. That's the little one with the moustache. And here we have a pilot's flying licence made out to Gerald Michael Powell, and some business cards advertising Powell's Pleasure Flights. Again a Tangier number."

"I told you the chap in the leather jacket was most likely a pilot," Goodhart commented. "He talked like a flyer."

Borrelli grunted and then looked at Larren. "It seems that you do not carry any means of identification. That in itself seems significant. But what is this?" His face wrinkled and he held up the homing receiver that Aziz had found in Larren's pocket. For a moment his face was blank, and then Khalil strode forward and took the receiver from him. He stared at it and his face became hard. His long fingers moved the switch, and immediately the loud bleep of the transmitter signal was heard. The pointer on the receiver dial swung towards the two watching men in matching lightweight suits.

"So — you led them here. One of you is carrying a homing device which they have been following. They must have trailed the Cherokee all the way back from Tangier."

The two men shifted nervously. "There is some mistake," the taller of the two said defensively. "This is not possible."

Borrelli had already covered them with the machine pistol. "You damned fools," he snarled. "Take your hands out of your pockets. Quick now. And bring them out empty. Aziz, you'd best search them as well."

"This is crazy," the taller man said. "We do not —"

"Shut up, Ricard. Do as you're told."

The tall man flinched, and slowly drew his hand from his jacket pocket. His companion followed suit and they both stood stiffly as Aziz moved behind them and emptied the contents of their pockets. It was on the second man that he found Chevalier's heavy gold cigarette lighter.

Khalil picked it up and broke it open. He pulled the wadding from inside and the miniature transmitter fell out on to the table. He looked at Borrelli.

"All right, Hassim." Borrelli's voice was savage. "Where did you get it?"

Hassim had backed away a step, and there was a knot of fear strangling his voice as he answered.

"I found it on the body of Henry Mallory, the man you ordered us to kill. You said that we must leave no means of identification on the body, and so I kept it. How could I know that there was anything inside?"

"You were told to destroy any means of identification on the body, not to loot it like a common thief. This thing was a plant and you fell for it. You've endangered us all just for the sake of a bit of petty pilfering on the side. I ought to —"

Borrelli never finished, for the bark of an automatic cut him short, and the man he was threatening staggered back and toppled sideways to the floor, a red hole neatly blotting out his left eye. The big man turned and saw that Khalil had picked up Hassim's own gun from the pile of effects that Aziz had placed on the table beside him.

Khalil said flatly, "That is the reward of a fool. For one fool working inside the organisation is more dangerous than a dozen clever men working from without." His voice only slightly betrayed the inner fury that had caused him to undertake his own killing, and his eyes were on Hassim's partner as he spoke.

Ricard swallowed hard, and his words came thick and rushed. "I didn't know, Mr Khalil. Hassim did not tell me that he had kept back that cigarette lighter. Mallory had a false passport, and we gave that and his wallet to our car driver in Tangier and told him to get rid of them. I thought that Hassim had given him the cigarette lighter also."

There was a moment of silence as Ricard's life hung in the balance, and then Khalil turned away and dropped Hassim's automatic back on to the table. Again he was as calm as if nothing had happened. He no longer spoke through Borrelli, but addressed Larren directly.

"I think that now I understand. You are obviously English, some kind of agent or policeman. When your people destroyed our British section they must have discovered something that told them that the man Mallory had escaped to Morocco. You were sent after him, and the fact that he had also hidden himself from us on arrival gave you a chance to find him before we did. You planted this homing device, either in the hope of following Mallory himself, or because you guessed that his murderers would be unable to resist such a valuable item if he was to be killed. Then you followed Ricard and Hassim here to Algeria." He paused. "Is my reconstruction approximately correct?"

Larren met his eyes for a moment, and then answered, "It sounds plausible."

"At least you do not deny it." Khalil frowned and then continued, "I think perhaps I have spared the wrong man. The loss of your friends has not made you as co-operative as I had hoped. Yet on the other hand, I think that you must know more than the other two would have been able to tell me."

Larren shrugged. "There's nothing left to tell. You've guessed it all."

"Not all," Khalil returned softly. "I cannot guess at whether or not you were able to leave a trail behind you that would enable more of your friends to trace you to this airfield. I cannot even be sure that there were only three of you, and we have yet to find the plane in which you arrived. With all these things you can help me."

"My amnesia," Larren reminded him. "You shouldn't have given me such a violent shock."

Khalil drew a long deep breath, but then Peter Goodhart interrupted boldly. "Their plane is somewhere to the north-west. In fact, I should expect to find it somewhere behind those red rock hills in the desert." Khalil was looking at him hard and he explained, "They approached the airfield from that direction, and in any case they couldn't land a plane just anywhere in the sand dunes. They would have to set her down upon solid ground, and the area around those hills is the only possible place within walking distance."

"But of course," Khalil smiled. "I should have realised. And naturally it must be behind the hills, because we know that it followed the Cherokee and must have arrived in daylight, when we would otherwise have seen it."

Borrelli said quickly, "I'll take the Land Rover, Mr Khalil, and a couple of men. We'll circle behind those hills and see what we can find."

"No," Khalil said sharply. "You are area controller and I may need you here. Ricard can redeem himself by attending to the plane. If there is anyone there bring them back, but in any case totally destroy the aircraft. Do you understand?"

"Yes, Mr Khalil." Ricard looked relieved at being given a definite job, and he came forward quickly to collect his automatic from where Aziz had laid it upon the table. He tried not to look down at his dead partner as he did so.

Borrelli detailed two of the armed men to accompany him, and Simon Larren watched their preparations with a sinking heart. He had hoped that Barbara Mallory would be left free to radio for help as soon as dawn arrived and no one had returned to her, but now he knew that he had been hoping for too much. There was nothing that he could say or do as Ricard and his two companions left, and he could only hope that his feelings were not showing on his face as he once again became the focal point of Khalil's attention.

The hook-nosed man pursed his lips thoughtfully for a moment, and then said, "I think we had best place this gentleman in cold storage until we know more fully the present situation. It will be best if we set a guard on both hangars until Ricard gets back to report, and you, Borrelli, will need to arrange such things. Later you will interrogate him for me and find out exactly how much or how little information he was able to leave for anyone who might follow. Meanwhile, see that he is made secure."

Borrelli nodded grimly. "Yes, Mr Khalil."

Larren was taken outside and marched across to another small building which proved to be an old detention block. It reminded Larren of an army glasshouse, and seemed to confirm the fact that the airfield was a relic from the Second World War. Now only the two hangars and the stone-built buildings that could not be dismantled remained, but the cell into which he was thrown looked as solid as when it had first been put into service.

Borrelli slammed the heavy steel door behind him, and Larren turned to watch through the grille as the big man twisted a large key in the lock. Borrelli grinned at him and threw the key to one of the two armed men who had accompanied him.

"That should keep you cosy," he said. "And I'll leave these two Johnnies to watch over you just to make doubly sure." He rapped some instructions in Arabic to his two subordinates, then slung his machine pistol over his shoulder and strode briskly away along the corridor.

Larren remained at the grille a moment, watching the two men. Then he turned away and surveyed the darkened interior of his cell. It was about ten feet square and totally empty; there wasn't even a bed or a bucket. In the far wall was a high barred window that allowed a little starlight to enter, but it was too high for him to see outside. He prowled around in the gloom, kicking the solid, immovable walls, and then he sat down with his back to the wall and tried to think.

For a while the cold anger inside him made his thoughts irrational, and he could not rid his mind of the picture of Chevalier and Powell lying together in a dead, crumpled heap simply because Khalil had reasoned that the shock would break Larren's own nerve. But then slowly he forced his mind on to the basic issue. There was no way of giving life back to two dead men. He had to concentrate on the problem of his own escape, and even more important, on finding some way of getting a report through to Whitehall and Smith.

He leaned his head back against the cold stone of the wall behind him, staring up at the blank ceiling of his cell, and then abruptly his thoughts fled and his mind became clear and listening as he heard a faint sound. It came again, and the second time he recognised it as human, or at least near-human, as though someone was moaning softly on the far side of the wall. He turned his ear against the stone, and then he was sure. There was someone in the next cell.

During the next half-hour the moans and movements became louder, as though the unseen prisoner was slowly awakening into pain or delirium. He began to mutter in rapid guttural sounds, and although Larren could not catch the words he recognised the language, for he had been obliged to learn German before he had been parachuted into occupied Holland so many years ago in 1944.

The movements from the next cell became even more restless, and Larren sat perfectly still as he tried to sift enough recognizable words to make a few grains of sense from the incoherent ramblings. And then suddenly the man's voice rose, sobbing and in perfect English.

"You can't do it. It's murder! It's mass murder … murder … *murder … MURDER!*"

The anguished voice rose in the heat of twisting fever, screaming the one accusing word over and over again. And then there was a commotion in the corridor outside the cells, the sound of a steel door crashing open, an angry scuffling on the far side of the wall, and then, mercifully, silence.

Larren rose to his feet and crossed to the grille in the door of his cell. He saw the two guards standing with their machine pistols in the lighted corridor, and then he saw Borrelli emerging from the next cell. The crop-headed man was tight-lipped, and in his hand he carried an empty hypodermic syringe with a long needle. He nodded to one of the guards to close the door, and then he saw Larren watching.

He said harshly, "He will not disturb your rest any more for tonight. But do not worry. It was not lethal, only a sedative."

Larren watched the big man hurry away once more, and his knuckles were white where he gripped the steel bars of the grille.

CHAPTER 16: A HOSTILE FRIEND

In the cabin of the old Fairchild Argus, Barbara Mallory was huddled against the sharp desert cold. It was over three hours since she had been left alone, and she had finished her weeping and remade her face. At first she had sat still and uncaring, feeling that it could not matter whether the three men returned or not, but now that the cold had penetrated she was hoping that the waiting would soon be over. Her thin blouse and the light jacket of her costume were ideal for the scorching heat of the day, but now she shivered as she hugged her folded arms to her breasts.

Through the cabin window she could see the dark silhouette of the hills showing clearly in the starlight, and from time to time she strained her eyes to see whether anything moved in the blackness. Mostly, however, she looked at the control panel and the cluster of switches and dials in front of her, for she was sitting in the pilot's seat. She felt no loyalty to the three men who had brought her here, and she knew that if she had been capable of flying the Argus on her own then she would have taken off and left them. Several times her hand touched the control column and the switches, but it was a false hope, and she knew that even if she started the engine she could only succeed in crashing the plane and killing herself. And despite her grief she had no thoughts of suicide.

The cold became more than a slight discomfort, and the constant sitting made her feel fidgety and restless. She shifted her position several times, and then abruptly decided that she didn't have to just sit here and do nothing. If she climbed up into the hills to meet the three men the activity would make her warmer, and as long as she did not go out of sight of the plane she could not get lost. The idea seemed to be healthier than to simply sit here brooding, and on impulse she pushed open the cabin door and climbed out. She hesitated for a moment, standing beneath the plane's wing and looking around her. Then she picked up her father's automatic from the seat, slammed the cabin door, and walked away towards the black barrier of the hills.

She climbed slowly and cautiously, the danger of falling reduced by the starlight which showed up the individual crags and boulders on the steep slope now that she was actually amongst them. She had seen the red rocks by daylight and knew that there was nothing here to harm her, and any basic fears of the night or loneliness were dispelled by the gun in her hand. She felt better for the exercise and was no longer shivering when she reached the top.

She paused, feeling a slight breeze ruffle her hair. Below her was the desert floor again, but there was no sign of anyone returning across the darkened dunes. She turned her head to look back at the Argus, standing like some squat, waiting bird, with more empty dunes beyond, and she was undecided whether to return or to go on. She did not want to go back and continue sitting in the cramped cabin, but at the same time she did not want to lose sight of the plane.

Suddenly she heard the faint sound of an engine, and her body stiffened warily. She turned her back on the Argus, staring out into the night on the far side of the hills. The sound was approaching fast, and after a few moments she saw the vague shape of a Land Rover clawing its way across the dunes. She thought for a moment that her three companions must have stolen the vehicle, but caution made her sink down on one knee to watch. The Land Rover passed close below her, and although there were three men inside she was sure that they were strangers.

The vehicle jolted out of her sight, seeking a way round the range of hills. The sound of the engine never faded completely, but when it gained in volume once more the sound was behind her. She turned, and descended the hill a little closer to the Argus, and then she crouched among some of the larger rocks and waited.

She saw the Land Rover reappear and rush up to the silent aircraft, skidding to a halt opposite the tailplane as the three men tumbled out. The leader of the three was a tall man in a European suit, and the way he held his right hand in front of him made it obvious that there was a gun in his fist. He yanked open the cabin door of the Argus and looked inside, and his companions — two men in long, nightshirt-like djellabas — halted behind him holding what looked like short, stubby little sten guns.

They held a short conference, and then the two men slung their weapons on to their backs and returned to the Land Rover. They fetched a heavy can from the back and pushed it into the cabin of the Argus, then one of them climbed inside and tipped the can up to spill its contents. The breeze was blowing in the wrong direction for Barbara to catch a smell of the fluid, but she knew instinctively that it was petrol. The Man climbed out of the plane's cabin, then the tall man struck a match and tossed it inside.

There was a muffled roar, and the front of the Argus exploded into a sheet of yellow flame. In an instant the hungry tongues were snaking along her wings and running down the slope of her tail. The whole plane blazed merrily, lighting up the frantic movements of her murderers as they hurriedly backed their Land Rover away from the glow. Then the plane's own petrol tanks ignited, and the tubby little Argus seemed to wholly disintegrate in a fearful blast of fire and sound, and black smoke gushed up to the stars from her ruptured remains.

Barbara had lowered her eyes, pressing her hands to her ears as the plane blew up, and she found that she was trembling violently. She crouched close to the earth for several long minutes, and when she finally dared to raise her face the smoking wreckage was burning itself out.

She looked for the Land Rover, and instinctively cowered back to the earth again, for the vehicle was moving slowly along the foot of the hills, and the two men in the back were gazing up the slopes, their eagle eyes searching every crack and crevice. She lay perfectly still, hardly daring to breathe and praying that the three men would not leave the Land Rover to search more fully. Twice she heard them cruise back and forth, but she did not lift her head again until she finally heard the engine accelerate as the vehicle moved away.

She straightened her back an inch at a time and peered down the slope. The twisted skeleton of the Argus still exuded a thick, slanting pillar of black smoke, and she uttered a silent prayer for the cold and the whim of fate that had caused her to leave it before the arsonists had arrived. There was no reason to descend to the scene, for there was nothing recognizable left, and so when she moved it was upwards, returning to the top of the hill. Barbara could still faintly hear the receding engine of the Land Rover, and when she reached the top she was just in time to see it disappearing back amongst the dunes.

She stood there, alone in the night now that the last echo of the Land Rover's engine had died. She was cold again now that the warmth of her earlier exertions had evaporated, and fear made her colder still as she stared out over the empty desert.

There was only one explanation for the sudden arrival of the three men who had fired the Argus, and that was that Larren, Powell and Chevalier had been caught and were now either prisoners or dead, and she could expect help from no one. She was truly alone.

She tried to think, but only one fact would stand clear: she could not stay here on the hilltop, for in daylight these crags would become a veritable oven of heat and she would soon die with the agonies of thirst. She had to move, and there was nowhere to go except to follow the Land Rover across the desert. It was a futile hope, but it was better than lying down to die, and she slowly descended the hill.

She walked out across the dunes until she found the tyre tracks of the Land Rover running across the sand, and then she walked between them and followed where they led. She was slower than the three men who had preceded her, and it was almost three hours before she came in sight of the old airstrip. She knelt wearily in the sand as she stared down at the silhouettes of the few stone buildings that remained, and felt the last of her hopes die within her. She had clutched to a dim belief that there might be a town or village at the end of her walk, where she might possibly find help as well as enemies, but now the delusion crumbled clear away.

For a long time Barbara stayed on her knees, feeling helpless and beaten, and then slowly her strength began to return. She tried to think again, re-sifting the harsh facts and searching for new hope. Her mind cleared gradually, and she realised that there was only one slim hope left: the hope that Simon Larren and his companions were not dead but merely prisoners. If that was so perhaps she could release them, and they in turn could help her. The odds against her success were remote, but it was the only possible way to her own salvation.

She sensed that it would soon be dawn, and that she did not have much time. Gripping tightly to the tiny automatic that was her only comfort, she began to move closer to the handful of buildings around the airfield control tower. She had been glad of the bright starlight that had bathed the desert throughout her walk, but now she began to wish that it did not reveal quite so much. Her heart was thudding painfully, and for the first time since she had looked down upon the dead body of her father she knew that she sincerely wanted to go on living.

She kept low, crawling on her hands and knees, tearing her stockings on the harsh sand. Several times she collapsed on her stomach with her face buried in the crook of her arm, rallying the courage to go on, and the automatic in her hand was like the straw of a drowning man.

She heard movements and voices in Arabic as she neared the buildings, but the fates were still being kind and no one saw her. The night sky was at last diminishing, and the stars were fading palely into greyness. Dawn was coming, and that was in Barbara's favour, for the guards that Borrelli had posted had relaxed their watchfulness and no longer expected any further infiltrations. Once two armed guards strolled by on a casual patrol only twenty feet away from her, but she lay flat behind the gentle slope of a dune and they did not even look around them.

She reached the wall of the nearest building and lay beside it in the sand, scared, and still not quite believing that she had got here unseen. Her body was tensed for the moment of discovery and she expected it at any second, but there was no uproar of alarm. She drew another breath to bolster up her weakening resolution, and then inched her way to the corner of the wall and looked round.

She saw another pair of armed men crossing towards the control tower, and quickly pressed her face to the sand. When she looked up again they had gone and she was able to study the buildings closest to her. One was a long block with a line of three tiny barred windows just below the level of the roof, and the sight of the bars immediately suggested cells. If any of the three men who could help her were alive, then that was the place to look. She glanced around to make sure that there was no one in sight, and then took the wild risk of scrambling to her feet and running openly across to the cell block.

She had lost her earlier sense of caution and her heart was pumping at almost double its normal speed. Daylight was approaching so swiftly that it frightened her, and she knew that if she was to do anything at all then she would have to achieve it quickly before her courage failed completely. She turned the corner of the cell block, and again luck was with her and there was no one to give the alarm. It was too late for hesitation, and she moved straight to the door. The centre panel of the door was made of horizontal wooden slats and one of them had broken away. She peered through the slit that was left and saw two guards squatting on the floor of the corridor outside the line of three cell doors. They were silently smoking cigarettes, and their machine pistols were propped against the wall behind them. Her sense of logic told her that nobody would be guarding the cells unless there were prisoners inside, and so she pushed the door open and thrust her automatic towards the squatting men.

"Hands up!"

The words sounded so shrill and ridiculous that it did not seem possible that they would be taken seriously. The guards stayed squatting and stared at her in amazement, and if either of them had laughed or even smiled she would have dropped the gun and burst into tears. And then, slowly and nervously, both guards raised their hands in the air.

Barbara was almost as surprised at their meek obedience as they were to see her burst in, and a little of her courage returned. She shut the door behind her and came farther into the corridor, and then she saw Larren's face appear abruptly behind the grille of the first steel door. Her voice cracked as she waved her automatic at the nearest guard and forced herself to speak again.

"Open that door. Release him."

The man hesitated. He licked his lips nervously and looked into her face, then back at the gun. Then slowly he straightened up. He reached inside his djellaba and she watched every move of his hand until he produced a large key. He licked his lips again, still without speaking, and then he stepped forward to unlock the door.

Larren came out fast, pushing the man backwards and snatching up both the machine pistols. He slung one across his shoulder by its strap, and levelled the other at the two guards.

"Thanks, Miss Mallory," he said warmly. "Thank you very, very much."

Barbara Mallory did not answer him, for she had slumped with her back against the wall and closed her eyes. The automatic in her hand dangled at arm's length, and she was sobbing silently with relief.

CHAPTER 17: THE FEARFUL TRUTH

Larren glanced over his shoulder and realised that the woman had carried out the last stages of his rescue on fraying nerves that had now collapsed, but for the moment he could spare no time for her. He couldn't afford to lose all that she had gained by turning his back on the two guards.

He jerked the machine pistol and motioned them into the cell that he had just left. They went nervously, shuffling past him and flinching as they saw the steely fixity of purpose in his grey-green eyes. Larren followed them into the cell and ordered them to face the far wall, and then he struck each one a vicious but accurate blow with the butt of the machine pistol. Their tightly knitted little skull caps gave them no protection and they toppled in an untidy heap to the floor.

Larren looked at them with satisfaction, and then turned to find that Barbara had recovered some of her composure and was watching him from the doorway. Her eyes were glazed with fresh horror and she said weakly, "Was that — was that really necessary?"

"They've killed both Chevalier and Powell," he told her grimly. "Cut them down in cold blood exactly as they did to your father. Do you still think that I should have spared them any sympathy?"

She stared at him. "But why? Powell was only a pilot. All he did was bring you here. Why did they kill him and leave you alive?"

There was an accusation of injustice in her voice, and Larren knew that she would have preferred to have found him dead, and Gerry Powell still alive. At least she had considered the pilot human. The fact struck a cold note inside him, and he realised that even in this precarious situation her feelings towards him still mattered.

He said quietly, "The man in charge here wanted one of us left alive to talk, and I was the lucky one chosen. He killed the other two in front of me because he thought that that would soften me up and make me easier to handle."

She looked into his face and then said almost bitterly, "But he picked the wrong one, didn't he? You haven't got a heart to soften."

Larren hesitated. "Let's just say that I've had previous experience of this sort of thing," he said at last.

Barbara lowered her gaze, and there was no time to waste on any further conversation. Larren turned away from her and knelt over the two unconscious guards, searching through their robes until he found two more keys on a ring.

"There's a man in the next cell," he explained briefly. "He was delirious last night, but I think he must know what's going on. I've got to try and talk to him."

Barbara said nothing, but stood aside as he went past her into the corridor. She followed and watched as he unlocked the door of the next cell, and finally she followed him inside.

This time there was a bed in the cell. It was close against the wall and supported a huddled shape covered by a dark brown blanket. Larren pulled the blanket aside and looked down on the grey, sweat-stained face of a very sick man. He looked to be about sixty, his hair had thinned to a few straggly lines of grey plastered to his scalp, and his unshaven face was thick with stubble. His eyes were closed and he breathed heavily in a drugged sleep. Larren's face tightened grimly, and after a pause he threw the blanket right back. He saw then that the man's left trouser leg had been cut away, and that there was a blood-stained bandage bound tightly around his thigh.

Larren glanced at Barbara. "Did a party of men destroy our plane?" he demanded.

She nodded. "They burned it. It got so cold sitting in the cabin that I walked up the hill to see if there was any sign of you or the others; that's how they missed me."

Larren looked down at the sick man again. "Then there's no point in my trying to carry him anywhere. There's nowhere to go. You'd better go back into the corridor and keep watch while I try to revive him. Can you do that?"

Barbara looked uncertain; she had her nerves under control once more, but she was still scared, and she realised that although she had found and released Larren her troubles were far from being over. It was now broad daylight, and their escape seemed impossible, and even the hard experience of Simon Larren could not work miracles. Then she nodded dully, and tightened her grip on her little automatic as she returned to the corridor.

Larren immediately started work on the unconscious man on the bed. He still did not know how he was going to pass on anything that the man might be able to tell him, but it was pointless to have got this far and then try to make his escape without knowing what was happening.

He had to treat the man roughly, pulling and shaking him, and slapping repeatedly at his face. The man groaned and twisted, but showed no signs of coming out of his oblivion. Larren began to sweat and cursed softly between his teeth. He worked for five continuous minutes and then gave up, facing the fact that Borrelli's injection had been one hundred per cent effective. The sick man would stay in his deep slumber for another two hours at the very least.

Wearily, Larren straightened up and stood back from the bed. He was convinced that the wounded man's feverish ravings of mass murder were connected with the stolen Scimitar and the two deadly Bullpup missiles, but there was no way of bringing the man round before Borrelli's drug wore off. He had to plan another move.

He stood undecided, and then abruptly Barbara Mallory reappeared behind him. "There are two men coming this way," she said flatly. "It looks as though they might be coming to relieve the two guards you knocked out."

Larren grimaced and swiftly replaced the blanket over the man on the bed. Then he snatched up his machine pistol and moved into the corridor. Through the missing slat in the door at the far end he could see the two men approaching across the sand.

His brain raced desperately. He could cover them as they came through the door, and then ensure their silence as he had done with the first two guards. But that would only give him a few more moments in which to think, for when the original pair who should have been relieved failed to appear, Borrelli would become suspicious and send more men to investigate. However he played it, he could not stop the alarm being raised in the next five minutes.

There was only one possible thing to do. Larren quickly locked the second cell door, and then hustled Barbara along to the third cell at the end of the block. He opened this door and pushed the woman inside, slipping in behind her and shutting the door with only seconds to spare. He pressed her back into the corner, warning her into silence, and waited with the machine pistol at the ready.

He heard the creak as the outer door was pushed open, and then puzzled comments in Arabic as the two newcomers saw that the corridor was empty. A sharp shout followed as the first arrival noticed the open door of the nearest cell, and their sandalled feet slapped swiftly on the concrete floor as they ran forward. There was another burst of excited jabbering as they found that Larren had vanished and that the two guards were sprawled senseless on the floor, and then one of them hurried away, shouting to raise the alarm.

In the third cell Larren kept well back from the barred grille in the door, and waited until he heard the guard returning with more men at his heels. Their voices were loud and agitated as they burst back into the corridor outside, and amongst them was the angry, cursing voice of Borrelli.

Larren turned his head and saw Barbara's frightened face peering up from the gloom behind him. He made a downward motion with his hand and she understood. She crouched low with her shoulders crushed back into the corner, and he could feel her trembling as he knelt and his own body pressed against her.

Outside, Borrelli swore the chattering men into silence and snapped harshly, "Ricard, get over to the main hangar and warn Goodhart and his team. Tell him that the prisoner is loose somewhere and that he just might try to sabotage the Scimitar. Then get a search party organised and get back to those hills where you destroyed that plane; it's just possible that he expects the plane to be still there. I'll organise a search of the other buildings. And make it fast — when Khalil finds out about this there'll be trouble."

Larren heard Ricard make a brisk acknowledgement and then hurry away, and then Borrelli's heavy footsteps came nearer down the corridor. Larren's hands were moist with sweat as he gripped his machine pistol, holding the short, sten-like gun close against his hip, and he stared up at the steel grille in the door. Discovery was imminent and his heart hammered. He had miscalculated and Borrelli was smart enough to check the third cell, and in a moment he would be making his last hopeless stand. Then Borrelli's footsteps stopped, and he realised that the big man was checking on his second prisoner.

"Well, at least Hegler is still here," Borrelli said harshly. "That's something. Our runaway friend must have been more concerned with saving his own neck than with anything else."

Larren heard him rattle the door of the second cell, checking that it was still locked, and then he turned away and went back to the first cell in the row. "Aziz, get a couple of the boys to carry those two stupid sleeping beauties over to the first-aid hut. Chuck some water over them and try and bring them round. Someone must have helped that spying Johnny to escape, and I want to know how it happened."

There was the sound of shuffling as the two unconscious guards were picked up, and then the movements in the corridor faded away as Borrelli and his men left the cell block. Larren gave them a few minutes to get well clear, and then he looked at Barbara and touched a cautioning finger to his lips as he rose to his feet. He ducked underneath the barred grille to reach the other side of the door, and then straightened slowly and silently to peer out into the corridor. Only then did he allow himself a soft exhalation of relief, for the corridor was empty. Borrelli had not bothered to post another guard over the sick man in the middle cell.

He helped Barbara to rise and said, "It's okay. Borrelli thinks I've bolted into the desert, so for the moment we've got a respite. He can't know how long a start I might have had, so he'll make a wide search. That should give us some time to think before he realises that we must be right under his nose."

She looked doubtful. "Those guards you knocked out will be able to tell him that it was already daylight when I released you. He'll know you can't have got far."

Larren smiled grimly. "Don't worry your head about that. After the crack I gave them they'll both be sleeping for a long time yet, and even when they do come round I wouldn't like to bet that they haven't got concussion."

She looked down at her feet and said in a low voice, "Even so — what can we do now?"

Larren leaned against the wall and smiled wryly. "For a while we'll just sit tight, until Ricard and a few more get themselves nicely spread out over the surrounding desert. That should reduce the odds a little. Then I'll make another attempt to get our friend talking. After that we'll play it by ear." He patted the machine pistol and finished, "With luck and with these to help us, we might be able to make a dash to the hangar where they're keeping the Cherokee that led us here."

Hope flickered in her eyes. "Could you fly it?"

"No," he admitted. "But we could hold them off long enough to use the radio."

"But that won't help us, will it? When they do take us we'll be killed. Whatever happens, we're dead."

He saw the beaten look come back into her eyes and she turned away. Her profile and the red lustre of her hair were an exact reminder of Andrea once more, and stirred a protective instinct that was deep in Larren's heart. He rested the machine pistol against the door and gently turned her to face him.

"I'm sorry, Barbara." It was the first time he had used her real Christian name. "I wish I could offer you some kind of real hope to cling to. And even though there isn't I still have to try and use that radio." He went on to tell her about the stolen strike-fighter, and everything he knew about the organisation that planned it, and he finished earnestly, "So you see, even though I don't know exactly what they intend to do, I do know that it's something evil that's going to cost an awful lot of lives. Just as it's already cost the lives of Powell, Chevalier and your father. Not to mention Sir Howard Davies and the group that planned his assassination in England."

She listened in silence, and then said slowly, "I think I understand. I'm sorry if I sounded selfish before. I'll try and help you if —"

She didn't finish, and they both stood listening as they heard the distant roar of an engine starting up on the airstrip. Larren snatched up his gun and rushed out into the corridor. There was a window in the far wall and he moved towards it until he could see out. Barbara came up behind him, and he felt her shoulder rub against his own. Through the window they both watched the smart little red-and-white monoplane taxi slowly along the runway two hundred yards away. She was moving away from her hangar and as they watched she gathered speed and took off into the glaring blue sky.

"Damn," Larren said softly. "They must be using her in the search. That's a possibility I had missed."

Barbara turned away, her hazel eyes once more reflecting the blackest depths of despair. "So that's that. Now you can't possibly hope to use her radio. We're finished."

"Not exactly." Larren was a man to whom only death meant defeat. "They're sure to bring her back by nightfall. If we stay free we can try then. Meanwhile let's have another go at reviving Hegler, or whatever it was that Borrelli called him."

He didn't wait for her answer but turned to unlock the door of the middle cell. Barbara stood silent for a moment, and then she looked through the window again to watch the Piper

Cherokee wheeling away in the sky. Finally she straightened her shoulders and followed Larren into the cell.

The man on the bed was still sleeping deeply, and there was nothing they could do but wait.

For the next nerve-racking hour they stayed in the sick man's cell. Outside they could hear shouted voices in Arabic as Borrelli's search parties combed the remaining buildings, and several times the searchers passed close to the cell block. Each time they came near Larren and Barbara froze into silence, and they could only pray that no one would think to look in the cell block a second time. Finally the activity became less and less, and the hope that Borrelli might now be satisfied that he had escaped into the desert gave Larren fresh confidence.

He went out into the corridor, moving carefully as he looked through the window and then through the broken slat in the door. The search parties appeared to have been called off, or spread farther afield, and he thought that now was the time to concentrate on Hegler. The man had stirred and muttered twice in the last fifteen minutes, and it was now possible that he could be brought back to consciousness.

Again Larren treated the man roughly, shaking him by the shoulders and continuously slapping his face. The grey head jerked back and forth across the pillow and the man began to moan feebly. Barbara winced as she watched, but she made no attempt to interfere. Larren repeated the man's name over and over again, as loudly as he dared, calling upon him to wake up. The man's body began to twist and his mutterings became louder.

For another full ten minutes Larren kept up the steady rain of slaps and entreaties, and then the sick man's eyes opened. They were weak blue eyes, staring blankly from the worn, lined face. His mouth quivered but no words came out, and Larren slowly lowered his hand which had been poised for another blow.

"It's all right, Hegler." He spoke gently, for he could afford to be gentle now. "We're friends. We've been trying to bring you round, that's all. Borrelli gave you some kind of a knockout drug."

Barbara came closer. She said nothing, but smiled faintly, and her presence seemed to reassure the man on the bed. He looked from one to the other, and then squeezed his eyes shut as though straining to gather his thoughts from the drugged corners of his mind. When he opened them again his throat worked and he said weakly, "Who are you?"

"My name is Larren. I'm an agent for British Counter-Espionage. I'm working against these people who are holding you here."

"You are working against the Assassins For Peace?"

Larren said slowly, "A.F.P. — Assassins For Peace. So that's what it stands for."

"You mean you did not know? You do not know what they are going to do?" The sick man's body moved convulsively under the blanket and his hand grabbed at Larren's wrist like a bony claw. He pulled himself up and babbled feverishly, "They are going to murder … murder … it will be wholesale murder!"

"Easy now. Easy." Larren steadied the man and pressed him back on the bed. "Tell me about these Assassins For Peace. Who are they? And what is their purpose?"

Hegler looked at him wildly, struggling against the restraining pressure of his hands, and then slowly the fever faded in his eyes and sanity returned. He lay back and spoke slowly and hoarsely, as though reciting a lesson that had been carefully learned in the hope that somehow, somewhere, this moment would come.

"The Assassins For Peace are an organisation of fanatics. It has a high council of five of the wealthiest men in Europe. Each has made so much money that the making of more money has become irrelevant, and so now they have sworn to make a better world. They believe that the United Nations and similar organisations have failed utterly, and that the responsibility for that failure must be shared equally by all of the world leaders who have refused to put aside national prestige in favour of world peace. And so they have decided to destroy those heads of state and heads of government, and destroy them in such a way that the men who must take their places will never be able to forget.

"When it is done the Assassins For Peace will announce their reasons for the act, and warn the new world leaders that the organisation still exists to exact more selective retribution from any of them who still does not heed the initial demonstration of their power. Any president or prime minister whom they feel is still fermenting hot wars or cold wars, or any national hates or prides, will be marked down for individual assassination."

Hegler's eyes closed and his head lolled back on the bed as he finished speaking, and at first Larren thought that he had collapsed. Then he saw that the man was merely trying to rally his crumbling strength in order to go on talking, so he said, "I already know about the Royal Navy strike-fighter they've stolen. And I know how they got away with it. When you're ready, try and go on from there."

Hegler lay silent for a full minute, and then opened his eyes once more. "You know about the Scimitar. It was because of the aircraft that they needed me. My name is Hegler, you know that somehow. I am a German. A technician. I was working for the Nasser government in Cairo when I was kidnapped by two men named Hassim and Ricard. They brought me here. They needed someone to supervise the fixing of extra long-range tanks to the Scimitar, and also to carry out routine maintenance on the aircraft itself, as well as checking over the rocket motors of its missiles. I was capable of those tasks, although how they came to choose me I did not know. I worked for them until I found out what they planned to do. When I learned the truth my own life became unimportant and so I tried to escape. Hassim and Ricard were sent after me. I was shot in the leg and brought back here."

Larren had already guessed the answer to the question he asked next, but he had to hear the answer from Hegler's own lips. His face was bleak, and there was cold dread freezing his stomach as he demanded harshly, "What are they going to do with the Scimitar, Hegler? How are they going to use those two Bullpup missiles?"

Hegler's eyes were sick with pain and fear. He said slowly, "The assassination of the British Prime Minister was only the first step. Every crowned head in Europe, and every world leader of importance, will be gathered in London for his funeral. They will all be massed together in St Paul's Cathedral for the final service — and that is the Scimitar's target."

Larren knew that the man on the bed was not lying, and slowly another fact registered, one that Hegler possibly had not realised. For this was Saturday and the funeral service would be taking place in London in a matter of hours. And even as the full horror sunk home into his mind they heard the thunderous roar of the Scimitar's two powerful turbojets reverberating across the desert airstrip.

CHAPTER 18: TO STOP A NIGHTMARE

On the runway the Scimitar stood like a chained arrow, her brakes holding her back as the blast of her engines rolled waves of deafening sound through the still, heat-heavy air. The whole aircraft trembled as the twin jets warmed up, and then the roar became louder as she moved down to the far end of the runway. She turned a full circle, then stopped, the engines dying to a throaty snarl. For five minutes she stood there, and then abruptly the engines swelled in volume once more. She moved slowly, then faster, and then her jet exhausts glowed scarlet as she thundered down the runway at full thrust. Her nose lifted and then she was airborne, streaking upwards at the rate of ten thousand feet per minute, like a glittering bullet aimed at the sun.

Simon Larren watched her go, powerless to stop her. He watched her climb into the blinding blue of the sky until his narrowed eyes could bear no more and he was forced to turn away. Barbara Mallory was gripping his arm but he barely felt the frightened pressure of her fingers as he listened to the Scimitar receding northwards. He was conscious of only one thing, and that was that unless the Scimitar was stopped she would be over London in approximately three hours, and in three hours the funeral service for Sir Howard Davies would be taking place beneath the great dome of St Paul's.

He shook his head, opening his eyes and blinking rapidly in an effort to clear his vision, then stumbled back into the cell where Hegler still lay upon the bed. Barbara followed him in from the corridor, and watched as he knelt by the sick German.

"Hegler," he said harshly, "is it possible? Is it possible that Goodhart can get through without being spotted?"

Hegler nodded weakly. "It is possible. He will fly north into the Mediterranean, then cut across the narrow neck of Spain and out into the Bay of Biscay. Then he will turn up the English Channel before crossing the south coast of England. Even allowing for the slightly zigzag course the distance is still a little less than one thousand five hundred miles, and with the extra fuel tanks I helped them to fit, that is within the Scimitar's range —" He broke off into a fit of painful coughing, but when his throat had cleared he struggled on. "His biggest danger is that he may be picked up by radar as he crosses Spain, but he will fly at maximum altitude, and if he escapes detection there then nothing can stop him. If he is spotted crossing the English coast then there will be confusion because he is flying a British plane. He can bluff any call to identify himself for the few vital minutes it will take for him to get through any coastal defences."

Larren still did not want to believe it. He said roughly, "But what about Goodhart? How does he expect to escape after he's released the Bullpups? He'll have flown the plane to its limit."

Hegler looked very weak, but he rallied himself once more to answer. "Goodhart is insane. He does not really care whether he comes back alive or not. He will bale out over the east coast and let the plane dive on into the North Sea, and then try to reach some pre-arranged rendezvous where the A.F.P. will pick him up."

The German's voice had sunk lower and lower as he talked, and now it trailed away altogether. Larren recognised the effort that Hegler had made to keep talking, and now he nodded his head in final acknowledgement and then turned away. He had no more questions, only the crushing problem of how to pass on a warning.

Hegler watched him for a moment, then his head fell slowly to one side. His eyes closed as his face pressed against the soiled mattress of his bed, and he sank slowly back into the oblivion from which he had been roused. Barbara moved closer to him and felt his pulse and temples. Then she said, "He's passed out again. He's running a high temperature."

Larren was staring bleakly at the far wall, but after a moment the words registered and he turned back to face her. He looked down at Hegler and said, "Leave him. He's told us all he knows, and there's nothing that we can do to help him. I dragged him back to consciousness before he had recovered from the effects of that drug, so now he'll sleep until it wears off naturally."

Barbara hesitated, and then stood up and came closer to him. Her previous hostility had faded, for she at last understood the kind of people they were fighting, and the fact that they had to fight them together. She touched his arm again and said, "Simon, how can we stop it? We *can* stop it, can't we? It's not only all those important heads of government — the Queen will be there as well, and all the royal family. The cathedral will be packed with people; and there'll be people outside as well — thousands of ordinary men, and women and children who have queued all night. Thousands and thousands of them. And he's going to fire those two rocket missiles! We must stop it, Simon. We must. *We must!*"

Larren clamped one arm around her waist, holding her fiercely as he shut off her outburst with his free hand. Her eyes were wide and distended in the gloom of the cell, and she writhed wildly in his grasp.

"Barbara, stop shouting," he hissed urgently. "Don't get hysterical." He waited until her eyes closed and her body became limp, and then he went on, "You've been wonderful so far, Barbara. You got me out of that cell and that gives us a chance, so just go on being wonderful for a little while longer. I haven't a hope of doing anything if you give way to hysteria."

She opened her eyes and nodded feebly, and when he took his hand from her mouth she said in a low, shamed voice, "I'm sorry, Simon. That was stupid and it won't happen again. But — but what are we going to do? What can we do?"

"We can be patient and lie low," he said grimly. "We'll stay here and wait; and hope and pray that that Cherokee returns before the next three hours are up. Because Peter Goodhart isn't the only one who can play at death or glory, and when that Cherokee lands I'm going to reach it and send a warning over the radio, even if I have to shoot down every man on this airfield to do it."

And so they waited; waited while the odds against them inexorably lengthened, and the vital minutes ticked gradually away into the lost labyrinths of time. The sun travelled its eternal scorching pathway across the blistering emptiness of the sky, and their seemingly airless cell became a sweltering oven of trapped heat. They both sweated freely, and most of the time they were silent, simply watching and waiting; knowing that each passing minute was carrying the stolen Scimitar and its deadly cargo anything from eight to ten miles closer to their ultimate destination.

There was still activity around the airfield, and the fear of discovery gave an added refinement of agony to their tautly stretched nerves. At any moment Borrelli could suddenly remember that he had not checked the third cell in his haste to organise the search for his missing prisoner; or Khalil, who must know the facts by now, might order him to search the whole of the airfield all over again. And that one or the other would inevitably happen was a foregone conclusion, for when the search parties started to return from the desert with negative reports then their two leaders would be forced to think again. Larren could only pray that the first to return would be the Piper Cherokee with its essential radio.

The first hour passed, and Larren calculated that Goodhart must be passing somewhere high above the Mediterranean coast of Spain, while in London the massed crowds lining the route from Westminster to St Paul's would be watching for the first glimpse of the slow-moving gun carriage that would carry the flag-draped coffin of Sir Howard Davies on his last earthly journey. Larren pictured the scene behind closed eyes, and tried to shut out the slaughter and horror that would ensue if Goodhart succeeded in loosing the two Bullpup missiles in the final stages.

The frustration of waiting went on, and for the tenth time Larren wiped the sweat from his palms and checked over the mechanism of the two machine pistols he had taken from the two guards. Each had a full magazine, and with speed and surprise on his side he was sure that he could shoot his way to the Cherokee if she returned to the airfield in time.

If the Cherokee returned in time.

The second hour lengthened towards the third and the strain increased. It was having its effect upon Barbara who was looking pale and ill, her face lined and wet with sweat, and somewhat tentatively Larren put his arm around her shoulders to steady her. She made no protest, and after a moment her head rested weakly against his shoulder. They stood with their backs to the wall so that Larren could keep watch on the corridor through the grille in the door, and briefly Larren looked down at her as he held her body against him. The auburn hair against his cheek made him feel that he was holding Andrea again, and he knew that he could love this woman in the same way if things were different. But things were not different, and he steeled his heart as he realised that the second hour was almost past, and that Goodhart must now be streaking out above the grey Bay of Biscay. If he had crossed Spain undetected, then the way was wide open.

Surely the Cherokee must return in time.

On the bed Hegler slept peacefully, no longer twisting or raving in delirium. It was as though the very act of telling his story had soothed him, and now that he had passed on the responsibility the awful burden had lifted from his conscience. Larren looked at him and envied him.

The minutes of the third hour began to peel away, falling into the irretrievable past, and slowly Larren tasted the black bitterness of despair. It was noon now and the stifling heat in the close confines of the cell was almost unbearable. Both he and Barbara had discarded their jackets, and now the back of her blouse was sodden where his arm pressed it to her shoulders. His own shirt was clinging to his back and he felt as though his mouth was coated with dry dust. They were both weary and thirsty. Larren still strained his ears to catch the first sound of the Cherokee's returning engine, but no sound came, and he finally faced the grim fact that the Cherokee was not going to return. At least, not in time to help them avert the nightmare that would be taking place in less than an hour.

Then Barbara raised her head and said hoarsely, "Simon, he's awake again."

Larren looked and saw that she referred to Hegler. The German had not moved, but the effects of Borrelli's injection had at last worn off and he had awakened as peacefully as he had slept. His eyes were open, and he was watching them with a blank lack of understanding.

Larren moved the woman and crossed over to the bedside. He said quietly, "How are you feeling?"

"I am all right." Hegler's voice was slow but clear. "My leg throbs, but I am accustomed to that. What is happening?"

"Nothing," Larren told him. "Goodhart must be two-thirds of the way to his target now, but there is nothing we can do until that Piper Cherokee gets back. And right now it's searching the desert for me."

"I see." Hegler closed his eyes, and then abruptly they flickered open again. "But I do not see. Why are you waiting for the Cherokee? Do you hope to fly away?"

"No," Larren said wearily. "But there will be a radio aboard her. If I can reach it I might get a warning through in time for the R.A.F. to intercept that Scimitar."

"But why wait for the Cherokee? There is a radio in the control tower."

Larren stared at him, and felt suddenly, incredibly foolish. "What did you say?"

"The control tower." Hegler looked puzzled. "Surely you must have realised that they have re-installed radio equipment in the control tower. They needed it to keep contact with their controllers in Zurich."

Larren remembered the powerful transmitters he had seen at the Sultry Strip, and then again at Larkspurs in Gloucestershire, and he cursed himself for his lack of thought. Of course there would be a radio in the control tower. It was obvious. It was so glaringly obvious, and he had been so totally blinded by the one all-obliterating thought of reaching the Cherokee that he had missed it. He felt weak with his own mammoth stupidity, and then relief replaced the weakness as he realised that even now it was not too late.

He swivelled round to face the woman and his unsmiling mouth barely cracked to let the words slip through. "Barbara, I'm a bloody fool, but there's no time now to stand here and kick myself. You'd better stay here with Hegler. I'm going to the control tower."

She drew a deep breath and caught his arm as he tried to push past her, jerking him round almost violently. "Simon, you can't go alone."

"It's my job. Of course I'm going."

"But not alone, Simon." She was in deadly earnest now, and there was a hardness in her that he had not seen before, a steadiness that surprised him. "You can't do it alone, you must know that. Even if you get to that radio you can't use it without someone to cover your back."

He stared into her face, and the steel shell around his heart began to crack and crumble away. He said harshly, "Not you —"

"Who, then? Hegler? He's crippled. He can't get off that bed. So it must be me." Her grip tightened. "Can't you see, Simon? It doesn't matter whether I'm a man or a woman, or even if I were a child. I can fire a gun and cover your back while you make that call — and you can't do it without me!"

Larren still stared at her, but despite the icy withering of his heart he knew that she was right. She drew her hand away, still looking at him, and slowly he unslung the second machine pistol from his shoulder. He held it out to her and said quietly, "All right, Barbara. Take it — and use it. If a man gets in front of us don't stop to think of him as a man. Just shoot him down. Remember that. Don't hesitate even for a fraction of a second to wonder whether he has emotions or feelings. There are no men out there — they're just cabbages. They're nothing but walking, soulless cabbages, but they'll kill you if you don't kill them first. Think of them that way, and you'll be able to do it."

She nodded slowly. "I'll remember, Simon. They're just deadly, filthy cabbages who murdered my father. I can do it."

Larren looked into her eyes and knew she would not fail him.

From behind them Hegler said, "Your only hope is to rush the most direct route. Go straight through the main door of the control tower. Inside there will be a flight of stairs to your left. The radio room is at the top. There will be guards on the door, and at least two men in the actual control room. How many more there might be on the ground floor I do not know. Only speed can get you through, and I can only pray for you."

Outside the cell block it was like stepping into a dry furnace. The distant sand dunes surrounding the airstrip shimmered like moving waves in a scorching haze of yellow heat. Above, the sun was suspended directly overhead in a molten ball of murderous white fire. Larren cringed as he felt its power, and for a moment he was blinded. He cursed softly, and then realised that this was no curse but a blessing. For the killing glare had driven all of Borrelli's men who remained on the airstrip into cover, and everywhere was hushed and still.

He glanced round at Barbara standing behind him in the cell block doorway. Her eyes were screwed up and squinting but she nodded bravely, holding her machine pistol close to her body. Larren drew a deep breath and they moved together, sprinting out into the merciless sunlight.

There were two buildings between them and the control tower, which was one hundred yards away, and they reached the first one panting and breathless, but unseen. Larren led the way quickly but cautiously along the wall, scrambling low on his knees to pass below the only window. He heard muffled voices from inside, but did not take the risk of raising his head above the level of the window sill to identify the occupants. He straightened up again at the corner of the building and felt Barbara pressing close behind him. The next building was the one-time briefing room where Larren had first been taken with Powell and Chevalier, and his face became even harder with the memory. Then he plunged out into the open again.

Barbara was close at his heels, and the dry sand spurted up from beneath their racing feet. Neither of them looked round. They ran as they had never run before, concentrating every effort into the sole need for speed. The wall of heat was an almost tangible barrier before them, and the golden ripples of sand seemed to snake across their path in a deliberate attempt to bring them stumbling down. At every second they expected to hear the first yell of alarm, and yet miraculously they blundered against the wall of the briefing room and the air around them was still pregnant with its silence. Larren's heart and lungs were straining to breaking point. His hands were slippery around his machine pistol and his face was streaked with streams of sweat. Barbara was even worse, and her breasts were lifting and falling violently beneath her soiled blouse, the ragged rhythm matched by the harshness of her breathing.

They froze for a moment, not quite believing that they were still undetected, and then they hurried on. Again they heard voices as they ducked low to get past the single window in the wall of the briefing room, and again Larren ignored them. Seconds later he was standing upright at the end of the wall, and now there was nothing between them and the control tower but a final forty yards of open sand.

The control tower was a long, two-storied building of red brick, with the actual, wide-windowed tower rising centrally above the main doors on the ground floor. Beyond it lay the empty concrete strip of the runway, reflected like a ruler-straight river of silver in the sun's glare.

Larren squinted at the open control-room doors, guessing that the guards must be just inside. Along the wall to his left was the door of the briefing room, and he knew that if he was spotted too soon he would be cut down between two sources of fire, and Barbara Mallory would be cut down with him. He faltered for the barest paring of a second, and then made his run for the control tower.

Again Barbara sprinted in his shadow, and they were almost halfway before the inevitable happened. There was a startled yell from the control-room doors and a guard appeared, frantically raising his machine pistol. Larren fired a snap burst from the hip that savaged the desert silence and the guard spun like a whirling dervish in a final dance of death. The dance ended as he crashed back in the doorway and fell, and Larren zigzagged desperately as he continued his headlong rush. Another machine pistol opened up and the burst of fire fanned past Larren's dodging figure as the second guard showed himself, and then Larren fired again and blasted the man down beside his partner.

Behind them there was uproar as men spilled out through the narrow door of the old briefing room. Larren ignored it, his mind fixed on gaining the control room, but Barbara Mallory twisted round, stumbling and almost falling as she ripped a burst of automatic death through the doorway, cutting down the leaders of the rush, and sending the others tumbling hastily back to safety. Then she wheeled and raced on.

Larren had already jumped over the two bodies sprawled in the doorway, and his shoulder crashed the right-hand door back against the wall as he skidded inside. He landed crouching on one knee and swept the machine pistol in a murderous arc, finding two horrified guards who died before they could level their own weapons to fire.

He looked left for the stairway and then dashed towards it as Barbara reached the doorway behind him. He hurled himself upwards and the swiftness of his assault took him up to the first landing before another figure appeared above him. Recognition flared in both their eyes, and the crop-headed Borrelli stared as he stood splay-legged at the top of the stairs. The dark-faced man in the windcheater jacket hesitated for one unbelieving second, a sten gun rigid in his hands, and that second cost him his life. Larren remembered Chevalier and Powell, and the promise he had made, and the killing lust blazed in his eyes as he cut Borrelli down. The big man's falling body tumbled past him as he surged on to the top of the stairs.

The door of the control room was wide open, and Larren entered in a headlong dive, slithering on his chest with the machine pistol gripped in both hands and stretched in front of him. There were two men inside, but the unexpected angle of his arrival took them by surprise and both hammered gunfire through the empty doorway above him as he crashed across the floor. He rolled on to one hip, and before they could lower their aim he had swept the machine pistol in a chattering circle, low enough not to damage the vital radio equipment, but high enough to shatter the legs of both operators at the knees. They screamed as they toppled over, and then Larren was scrambling up and kicking their weapons out of reach. One of them had fainted, and the other collapsed beneath a brutal blow from Larren's foot.

The control room was taken, and now he turned to look for Barbara. She was still on the ground floor, kneeling in the main doorway and holding off the wave of men converging on the building. She had had the foresight to snatch up the two machine pistols dropped by the dead guards, and these now dangled from her shoulder.

Larren hurried halfway down the stairs and yelled at her to join him. She turned, and in the same moment he saw her stagger and reel, clutching at her stomach with one hand. Larren fired a long, savage burst through the doorway above her head, and then threw aside his empty pistol and grabbed up the slightly larger sten gun that had fallen from Borrelli's dead hand.

He charged down the stairs, ignoring the furious storm of gunfire that was now coming from outside, and caught Barbara's lurching body before she fell. She shuddered against him and he sobbed and swore as he backed up the stairs, dragging her beside him. The sten in his right hand jittered wildly as he covered their retreat with clumsy one-hand bursts of fire.

He reached the control room again and helped her inside. He had to release her in order to drive back the first influx of men who tried to invade the ground floor, and then for a moment the hideous tumult of gunfire stopped. He turned then and saw that Barbara was half leaning and half kneeling against the wall. Her teeth were clenched and her face was white as a sun-bleached skull. She still held her pistol, but beneath the fingers of her left hand the blood was oozing redly from the wound in her stomach.

He lowered his sten and began to tear off his shirt for a pad, but she stopped him and said weakly, "No, Simon. There's no time. Use the radio while I can still hold them off. That's the only thing that's important."

Larren hesitated in anguish, but she shifted to where she could cover the stairs through the open doorway, and unsteadily allowed the two spare machine pistols to drop to the floor by her side. She looked up at him, and even in agony her voice was still resolute. "The radio, Simon. There isn't much time."

Larren turned away bitterly and hurried over to the radio transmitter. He jammed the earphones over his head as he sat down, and began speaking earnestly into the table microphone as he tuned the dials in front of him in search of a contact. Behind him there was the clatter of fresh gunfire as the men below launched a new attack, but Barbara still had the strength to hold them at bay.

Grimly Larren ignored the sounds as he hunted the wavebands, sending out an endless repetition of the international distress call. "Mayday … Mayday … Mayday … This is an emergency … Mayday … Mayday … Mayday…"

Behind him the battle raged more fiercely, and he could hear the screaming voice of Khalil fanatically urging on the attackers, and his own voice began to pitch higher towards frenzy as the minutes ticked away. He had to force himself to pause every few seconds to listen for an answer. The frustration inside him swelled to bursting point and his hands slipped clumsily as he fumbled with the waveband dials.

"Mayday … Mayday … Mayday … *For God's sake, this is an emergency* … Mayday … Mayday … Mayday…"

For five fruitless minutes he called out the same pattern of words while Barbara defended him from the gunfire below.

Stray bullets ricocheted into the control room and smashed through the wide glass windows on their way out, but none of them scored a lucky hit. He glanced back once at the woman crouching in the doorway, and knew that she was weakening fast, and then mercifully the earphones crackled against his head.

"Your Mayday received … Your Mayday received … This is a Royal Air Force transport aircraft flying between Gibraltar and Malta … Please identify yourself and state your position … Over."

Larren almost sobbed with relief, and then he recovered himself and rapped out his warning as clearly and as factually as he could. He identified himself and added his approximate position, and then he stressed that the Counter-Espionage office in Whitehall would be able to vouch for him. The distant pilot of the transport plane sounded incredulous as he asked quick questions, but the urgency of Larren's voice convinced him and he broke off to radio his base.

Larren stood up slowly and took off the earphones. The shooting had lulled again, as though somehow the men below had sensed that the message had gone through. Barbara was doubled up in the doorway, still holding on to her machine pistol, but when he touched her it dropped from her fingers and she slumped against the wall. There was blood all over the front of her blouse, blood on her hands and arms, and blood on the floor below her. But her face was empty of blood, and her breasts barely moved as she crumpled to the floor.

Larren laid down his sten gun, and gently cradled her head. Below there was silence. For the second time in his life emotion was choking his mind, and as he kissed her forehead he moaned softly, "Andrea. Not again, my darling. Andrea."

And then the light hazel eyes flickered open, and the auburn hair caressed his arm as she stirred her head. "My name is Barbara," she said feebly. "Not Andrea. Barbara." Even in death there was a moment of understanding, and she whispered, "Poor Simon. I'm so sorry."

Larren stared down at her closed eyes, and then suddenly there was a rush of feet on the stairs and gunfire blazed again as Khalil led the bravest of his men in a reckless charge. Simon Larren lowered the woman and almost slowly reached for his sten, and the renewed lust to kill thundered once again in his frozen heart.

CHAPTER 19: THE SKIES OF LONDON

In London it was another beautiful June day, and the pavements along Whitehall and the Strand, and leading up towards St Paul's, were massed with silent swarms of people. Most of them had waited all night with their blankets and their vacuum flasks, and now the moment of hushed mourning pageantry was near. The coffin had been carried from Westminster Hall where it had lain in state, and borne with slow, reverent ceremony to the waiting gun-carriage, and now it began its last slow journey. Overhead a flight of Royal Air Force Lightnings swept away after flying in close formation for the final salute, for Sir Howard Davies had been a fighter pilot during the epic Battle of Britain, and this was the final farewell from the sons of his former comrades. The roar of the fly-past faded high above the saddened heart of the great city, and then there was silence but for the dull rumble of the gun-carriage wheels and the firm measured tread of those who walked behind.

In proud but muffled splendour the procession moved away from Parliament Square, up towards Whitehall and the straight white monument of the Cenotaph. A faint breeze stirred the vivid Union Jack that draped the coffin, and somewhere in the crowd there was an audible sob of emotion. A million hearts were heavy, and a million eyes were blurred with unshed tears. The spectacle was solemn, yet moving, and even in death there was majesty.

Over a thousand miles away in the Mediterranean, the Air Officer Commanding at Air Headquarters Malta read a copy of the report radioed in by the pilot of one of his transport planes in flight to Gibraltar. His face paled, and although he prayed that this might be some fantastic hoax it could not be ignored. He gave orders for the report to be passed on to the Home Office as a matter of top priority.

At the same moment the pirate Scimitar was streaking at little more than wave-top level above the slow swell of the Atlantic, heading into the mouth of the English Channel on the last leg of her long flight. She had slipped unnoticed across the narrow neck of Spain before coming down from fifty thousand feet, and now the sea-grey colouring of her upper surface merged with the waves to give her maximum camouflage from any chance aircraft above. Sub-Lieutenant Peter Goodhart sat relaxed in the pilot's seat, and convinced himself that he was as good as home.

He was a skilful pilot, for he had taken advantage of everything that the Fleet Air Arm could teach him, and he was smiling as he approached his target. He did not see himself as the pawn of fanatics, but instead as a man of history and achievement. For once he had loosed the Scimitar's two missiles, then for better or for worse he would have changed the course of the world. He remembered what the dead pilot Powell had called him and his face twisted viciously, for after today no one would ever call him a mummy's boy again.

And that was the root of the mad spur that drove him on. His father had died when he was only four years old, and Goodhart had been brought up by a dominant and possessive mother. In everything he had ever done she had insisted upon being his helper and guide, spoiling every effort at self-achievement and stifling every move he made towards independence. At his first school she had arrived in passionate fury to chastise a headmaster who had caned him for some minor misdemeanour, and had so earned him the nickname of mummy's boy from classmates with less adoring parents. And the stigma had remained. Peter Goodhart had never been without a clean shirt and clean socks, but schoolboys are naturally grubby and he was often without friends.

At the college he later attended she had again been evident in the background with her excessive concern for his welfare, and again the mummy's boy label had been affixed. He could not escape her, and when he left college it was her money and influence that had provided him with a nicely suitable job. Her love had all the qualities of a leech.

Joining the Fleet Air Arm had been his own idea, and the only one that he had ever found the fortitude to carry out. His mother had been shocked and surprised, but with the tenacity of a bulldog her love had persisted. She was still there in the background and in her never-ending letters, a constant reminder. And so the damage was done, the warped tool was shaped, and unwittingly the Royal Navy had added the final polish and lethal skill that had made him the perfect pawn for those who used him now.

He had to do something, to achieve something, that was outside his mother's control; even outside the control of his naval superiors whose authority had partly replaced the affectionate chains he had come to loathe. He, Peter Goodhart, had to do something on his own, something world-shaking that would make him forever a man who was his own master. And now he had the power, now he had the opportunity. This was his flight to destiny.

He was well into the Channel now, and it was time to climb before he rammed some lumbering liner or cargo ship in the congested shipping lanes. His smile tightened and he stood the Scimitar almost on her tail as she strained up to her maximum ceiling. The sunlight dazzled against her white underbelly and the sleek Bullpups that nestled beneath her swept-back wings, and then she reached her top speed of over seven hundred miles an hour as Goodhart turned her towards the coast of England.

And above the City of London the sun still shone. The gun carriage and its escort had crossed Trafalgar Square; moving up the Strand where the packed pavements on either side were like still rivers of silent, grieving faces; on through Fleet Street, and then slowly up Ludgate Hill. Before the broad steps of St Paul's the cortège stopped, and the pallbearers came forward once more to lift their noble burden.

Inside, beneath the great central dome of the cathedral, the world had gathered to pay him homage. The great ones waited; the crowned heads of Europe; the leaders of countries and Commonwealth; presidents and premiers. Here, East mourned with West, for Zuchev of Russia stood side by side with the President of the United States. The iron-faced Russian wore the uniform of a Soviet air marshal, for he too had flown a fighter plane during the Second World War. It was this fact that had linked him to Sir Howard Davies, forming the bond of shared experience that had brought him personally to the funeral. It was also a bond which had eased international tensions since Zuchev came to power, and which the world feared might now be lost for ever.

And in Whitehall, in the great block of the Home Office, another air marshal was reading the hurried report that had just come through from Air Headquarters Malta. His face turned grey. For a moment he hesitated with the thought of contacting Counter-Espionage to verify the man Larren as a creditable source of information, but the delay could have been fatal. He assumed responsibility and grabbed for the telephone that linked him with Fighter Command.

Four minutes later a flight of six Hunter interceptor fighters streaked away from their base in south-east England. Armed with four 30mm Aden guns, and with air-to-air Firestreak missiles slung under their wings, they took to the sky like angry hornets. Had they been four minutes sooner they might have been in time, and the murderous Firestreaks with their infra-red heat-seeking warheads might have done their job. But although the Hunters could match the Scimitar for speed, Goodhart was already over England and homing on his target.

Hurtling above Surrey at maximum speed, Peter Goodhart never even knew how narrowly he had missed having a flock of vengeful Hunters meet him face to face. However, he did know that he had been spotted by coastal radar, for he had received and ignored a radio call to identify himself. The voice had been puzzled, and he had grinned with the knowledge that the fact that he was flying a British plane had left them confused. By now they would be panicking, but he had the valuable few minutes he had needed. He had dived fast immediately after crossing the coast, and he was again flying low level. He knew he was too low to be brought down by the Bloodhound anti-aircraft missiles that were Britain's standard defence, and he had too good a start to be caught by fighters.

He was three minutes from target.

In the high dome of St Paul's the first sad notes of the organ softly pealed and echoed; the service was beginning. The leaders of nations stood with downcast eyes. Outside the cathedral the vast crowds still waited, still silent, unmoving.

In the Home Office the grey-faced air marshal had aged a thousand years. Coastal Command had verified that a Scimitar strike-fighter was bearing down on London at attack speed, and he knew that the Hunters had been sent up too late to intercept.

But he still had one card to play. The flight of Lightnings that had formed the fly-past salute were still aloft, and the Lightnings were Britain's fastest operational aircraft, capable of supersonic speed of one thousand five hundred miles per hour.

Those last three minutes were the supreme climax to the whole of Peter Goodhart's frustrated life. His mouth was set in a tight smile behind his oxygen mask and his eyes gleamed with triumphant brilliance. He knew that after carrying out his mission he was almost certain to die, for he had never been quite fool enough to believe in the optimistic escape plan that the A.F.P. had mapped out for him. But he did not care. Only this moment of achievement mattered, and he knew that if it became necessary and the Bullpups failed, then he would crash-dive the Scimitar itself through the roof of St Paul's. He was both suicidal and insane.

The great, sprawling mass of London was before him, and ahead he could see the winding blue glitter of the Thames. It was the first time that he had ever seen the Thames looking blue; usually it was grey. In the June sunshine the whole city looked brighter and cleaner than it had ever appeared before, and he saw it as a good omen. The majestic dome of St Paul's showed clearly against the sky.

His hand moved to the switch that controlled the Bullpups. In a matter of seconds he would be within the two-mile range from which he could release them and guide them down. He took a last glance at the empty sky before concentrating on the cathedral, and then the smile froze on his face as he saw the six blurs of silver zooming towards him.

The Wing Commander piloting the leading Lightning put her into a howling dive as he saw the Scimitar below him, and the rest of his flight peeled off to follow him down. For the purposes of the fly-past the Lightnings had been unarmed, but heedless of this fact they closed with the pirate strike-fighter. If they could only buzz her off course and harry her for a few vital minutes, then the slower Hunters could catch up with their air-to-air Firestreaks.

In the Scimitar, Peter Goodhart screamed with almost childish fury. He recognised that attacking silhouette of the supersonic Lightnings and knew that he was hopelessly outmatched. His hand left the missile control switch, diving frantically back to the control column as he banked the Scimitar desperately to avoid the first descending fighter. His eyes screwed shut and his slender body flinched in expectation of the streaming cannon shells that would at any second tear himself and his plane to agonised shreds.

But no shells came. The Lightning swept past him with a flashing roar, missing him narrowly but without firing a shot. He opened his eyes and saw the second fighter zeroing in, but again there was no cannon fire as he swerved out of its path.

And then he realised the truth; the Lightnings were from the fly-past salute that had accompanied the funeral and carried no armament. He laughed then, and brought the Scimitar back on course for St Paul's.

The third Lightning hurtled down, but Goodhart held the Scimitar until the last moment before weaving to let the plane dive past. He had zigzagged several miles west of his target by now, but he knew that he could return now that the Lightnings had proved themselves relatively harmless.

For the next few minutes they fought a fantastic battle through the brilliant blue skies above south-west London. His courage had returned and Goodhart no longer hesitated to use his own 30mm Aden cannon to keep the Lightnings at bay. The seven planes weaved and tumbled in darting frenzy, the Lightnings circling and spinning as they attempted to force the Scimitar down without falling victim to her chattering guns. But through the crazed confusion Goodhart once more brought his sights on to the centre of the city beneath. His hand reached to release the Bullpups, and he aimed the nose of the Scimitar to follow them down.

The Wing Commander of the Lightning flight had climbed again, almost blacking out in his effort to regain his previous altitude in the shortest possible time. Now he knew that the armed Hunters would be too late, and that the close buzzing of his companions would not stop the Scimitar from achieving her purpose. Only the final sacrifice would stop her, and with a prayer the flight leader committed his soul to God, and his aircraft to a last supersonic dive.

Goodhart felt the crack as the plunging Lightning split the sound barrier, and for the barest atom of time he saw its attacking silhouette bearing down at fantastic speed.

Her nose was aimed at his cockpit and seemed to spear him directly between the eyes. And then, with a crack like magnified thunder, the two planes met and exploded into a shattered mass of black smoke and scarlet flame.

High above, the pilots of the surviving Lightnings circled, their faces white as they watched the molten remains of the two locked planes falling through a mushroom of smoke to the distant earth. From the south-east the distant specks of the unneeded Hunters appeared in the sky. And in the great cathedral of St Paul's the mourners of the world sang a final hymn.

CHAPTER 20: THE FINAL CONFERENCE

An hour after Simon Larren had made his desperate radio call, a plane loaded with Algerian troops landed on the single runway of the desert airstrip. Their government had been informed by Whitehall, and as their own president had been present at the funeral service in St Paul's Algeria's military leaders had been swift to act. The troops swarmed out of their plane and met with little resistance as they occupied the airfield. The grim-faced major in charge led a picked commando team in a direct rush upon the control tower, and in a short three-minute battle they had forced their way inside. The defenders had already lost their taste for fighting, and their leaders, a dark-faced man in a windcheater jacket, and a tall hook-nosed man in a pure white suit that was now stained with red, were lying dead at the foot of the stairs leading to the high control room.

The Algerian major hurried up the stairs, cradling an automatic rifle and with a group of his men close behind him, and then he halted in the doorway to the radio room. Inside a man knelt on the floor, close to the body of a woman. The man was still, his shoulders bowed with defeat, and he did not look up. Beside him lay an empty sten gun and four empty machine pistols, and the air around him was thick with the smell of cordite, blood and death.

The major turned and shouted a command, and a moment later an army doctor came running up the stairs. He pushed into the control room and rested his medical pack on the floor.

He knelt and then moved his head in a slow, negative gesture as he saw the amount of blood that the woman had lost from the ugly wound in her stomach. He did not have to feel for a heartbeat, and he looked at the man.

"I am sorry, Monsieur." He spoke in French, his voice quiet and regretful. "If the blood could have been staunched she might have been saved. If the bleeding could have been stopped in time."

Larren raised his head slowly and looked at the stranger before him. The words echoed emptily in his heart. *If the bleeding could have been stopped in time.*

He said bitterly, "I know — but there was no time."

He rose unsteadily to his feet, and the major moved to help him. He swayed, and shook his head as though in a daze, and then his dulled eyes focused on the major's face.

"I think you've got them all," he said. "Borrelli and Khalil, the two leaders, are both dead. The others lost heart after Khalil died in the last rush. A man named Ricard was the only other one capable of rallying them, and I think he lost his loyalty when they murdered his partner." He paused wearily, and then finished, "There's a sick man in the cell block named Hegler — he'll answer all your questions."

The major nodded, and began to issue a spate of orders. Two soldiers came forward to lift the dead body of Barbara Mallory, but Larren waved them away. He knelt again, gathering strength, and then he lifted her in his arms. He stood there for a moment before carrying her down the stairs, and when he spoke his voice was pained with despair.

"Why couldn't it have been me instead of her? I'm a killer — a butcher. I'm the mad dog they unleash when there are other mad dogs on the loose. Why couldn't it have been me?"

But the Algerian had no answer.

And later that day in Zurich the High Council of the A.F.P. held its final meeting. It was hastily convened in the top-floor conference room of one of the large office blocks that was owned by Raab, and once again it was the dapper white-haired man who had called them together, and who now took the chair. There were only four of them now, and the seat that should have been occupied by Khalil the Libyan was vacant.

As before Raab stood upright and perfectly controlled, his voice was calm and level. He addressed them as though conducting a meeting of mild shareholders in a well-established firm.

"Gentlemen," he said quietly, "I think you have all heard the news that has flashed around the world during the past few hours. Sub-Lieutenant Goodhart failed to carry out the mission we planned. His Scimitar aircraft was rammed in mid-air by a British Lightning. A noble act that has ruined a noble cause. Our Algerian section has been taken, and our good friend Khalil is reported to have been killed." He paused and then continued, "We have failed, gentlemen. Our organisation is smashed, and it is only a matter of time before today's events can be traced back to this room. What we have tried to do has set every country, every police force in the world against us, and even with our resources there is nowhere that we can run to. And in any case, I would not run. I could not spend the rest of my life in running like a hunted animal. Neither do I intend to suffer the indignity and dishonour of facing trial, and in all probability execution." He stopped and smiled wanly. "You will see, gentlemen, that I have also made provision for you."

He sat down slowly, and his three colleagues stared dumbly at the oiled and polished automatic pistols that lay upon the clean pink blotters before them. Their eyes had been held fixed by the neatly arranged firearms ever since they had entered the room, and even now they could not fully believe in what Raab was saying.

Then Lemmer looked up and said harshly, "But, Raab —"

He never finished, for Raab, still smiling sadly, was holding an automatic to his own temple. His hand was perfectly controlled, and carefully he squeezed the trigger.

The sight and the sound held the three transfixed, and they watched as their leader slumped slowly over the head of the table. Then Lemmer moved, heading blindly for the door, and Collard the Belgian rushed to follow him. Only Neumann remained, still staring uncertainly at the gun on his blotter.

The two who had fled blundered frantically down the stairs, ignoring the lift and scattering startled office workers aside as they were attracted by the sound of the shot. They were halfway to the ground floor when they heard the second shot, indicating that Neumann had followed Raab's example with Teutonic fortitude. The echoes spurred the two survivors on and they stumbled breathlessly into the lobby on the ground floor of the building. Lemmer was still in the lead, but it was there that he skidded to an anguished halt. Collard cannoned into his back, and then both stood resignedly still.

For through the wide glass doors that opened on to the street they could see two hefty Swiss policemen rushing determinedly to meet them.

A NOTE TO THE READER

Dear Reader,

I have written under other pen names and so my website is at **www.robertleaderauthor.com**. Go to my Robert Charles page for information on my Robert Charles thrillers. The website has a full biography, a travel blog and notes on how each book came to be inspired and written. Please pay a visit if you would like more information on Simon Larren or anything else I have written.

In today's publishing world online reviews are vitally important and if you have enjoyed my work please spare the time to write a review for **Goodreads** and **Amazon**, or just a complimentary mention on any media platform.

If you want to contact me you can do so through my website. I am always pleased to hear from readers. In the meantime I will get on with the next Falcon SAS novel for your enjoyment.

Sincerely yours, Robert Charles

SAPERE BOOKS

Sapere Books is an exciting new publisher of brilliant fiction and popular history.

To find out more about our latest releases and our monthly bargain books visit our website:
saperebooks.com

Printed in Great Britain
by Amazon

15509270R00119